The
Peep-Larssons
Go
Sailing

THE
PEEP-LARSSONS
GO
SAILING

BY EDITH UNNERSTAD

*Translated from the Swedish
by Lilian Seaton*

ILLUSTRATED BY ILON WIKLAND

THE MACMILLAN COMPANY, NEW YORK

The
Peep-Larssons
Go
Sailing

CHAPTER ONE

WE ARE KNOWN as the Peep-Larssons because of the time when we went around selling Peep saucepans, one summer a year or two ago. And last summer we went sailing. Heaps of lovely things happened then; it always seems as if the nicest things happen in summertime.

Papa is Peter Evert Patrik Larsson. He owns the factory where, among other things, he makes the famous Peep saucepan which shrieks when the food is ready.

Mama used to be an actress, but since we started coming into the world she has only been a housewife. There are seven of us children. Some of us have rather silly names, because before Mama was married, when she was on the stage she used to play Shakespearean roles, and she was determined to name all the girls after Shakespearean heroines. But it doesn't really matter. Desdemona, our eldest sister, who was sixteen when we started our sailing career, is called Dessi, Miranda, aged fifteen, is Mirre, and Ophelia, the two-year-old, is always known as Little O. Rosalind, the fourteen-year-old, has to put up with her full name.

We boys are Lars, Knut, and Pysen. I am Lars. Knut

was eleven, Pysen four, and I myself thirteen at the time.

Then we have an Aunt Bella, who has a she-cat called Persson. Aunt Bella lives in the same house in Norrköping as we do, and Persson is as often with us as with her.

Laban and Lotta are our horses. Since coming to live in Norrköping we often go to Aunt Bella's summer cottage in Vikbolandet, and then we turn Laban and Lotta out to grass. However, in this book we don't touch on any of that but go sailing out to sea, so it is only for form's sake that I mention these things.

The cottage is close to the bay of Bråviken, and that's where we young ones got a real taste for sailing. Because a near neighbor of ours is awfully good at it. He is manager of the dyeing department of a big weaving mill in the town, and he has been most decent to us all. It was he who taught us sailing aboard his beautiful *Tanja III*. He was very nice and not a bit snooty, though we didn't know the first thing about it to begin with, but kept getting in the way and hauling on the wrong ropes, as we say. Mama said she couldn't imagine where he got all his patience from.

However, but for him, Papa would probably never have decided to get a boat and allow us to go out in her all on our own. Because he himself is no sailor. He had been a commercial traveler all his life until he got this factory. And whenever he had a spare minute he was

always busy with his inventions and never had time for anything else.

For two summers we used to go sailing regularly in *Tanja III*. But the dye manager was old and ailing, and the doctor thought it time he began to lead a less strenuous life.

"The youngsters ought to have a boat of their own, you know," said Papa. "A sturdier, more solid one."

"One that couldn't capsize," said Mama, who is nervous about us and scared of the sea. "A sort of barge, for instance."

"*Barge!*" we exclaimed, we, who had sailed in *Tanja III*.

"But there isn't one to be had at the price we could pay," said Papa. "A sailing boat with room for seven aboard would cost a pretty penny."

"Seven!" protested Mama. "Pysen and Little O will stay at home."

"But I shall go sailing, oho yes," said Pysen.

"Better count on seven, anyway," said Papa. "Time goes so quickly and children seem to grow up all at once."

"I am big, oho yes," said Pysen solemnly. "Little O isn't, oh noho!"

He had taken to adding "oho yes," or "oh noho" to the end of every sentence. He was a person who knew his own mind.

"Couldn't you make us a cheap boat, Papa?" said Mirre. She thinks Papa can do anything. When we went to dig potatoes in Aunt Bella's vegetable garden, she said, "Can't Papa invent a fork for digging up the good potatoes and leaving the bad ones in the ground?" And when Aunt Bella, who is by way of being a bit hefty, wanted a new spring coat but thought the latest styles would make her look as big as a house, Mirre said, "Papa can invent a coat that will make you look like a mannequin." But he couldn't, you know. He laughed, now, and said that he wasn't a boat builder. No, we'd just have to make do for the present with a rowing boat, for there wasn't much hope of our ever getting a sailing boat.

After that for some time we heard nothing more of the subject. But one day, after he got back from a business trip, Papa dropped a bombshell.

I had an idea something was in the wind, for I had noticed that bits had been cut out of the advertisements for boats in the paper from time to time. All the same, it took our breath away when he announced, "Well, kids, I've bought you a boat!"

We absolutely *yelled* with excitement, I can tell you.

"A boat! Hurrah!"

"What's she like? What kind of boat?"

"Will there be room for all of us?"

"Patrik, dear, I do hope it isn't dangerous!" (Mama was the one who said this.)

"Is she a nice one, Papa?"

"How much canvas does she carry?"

"Can we go out in her on our own or shall we have to have grownups with us?" We crowded around, all asking questions at once. But he said, "Take it easy; don't hug me to death. The boat is no beauty and she certainly won't travel very fast. There'll be room aboard for all of you, though you'll be a bit cramped. On long trips you'd better take a tent for some of the crew."

Long trips! We looked at one another.

"Yes, Maja," Papa went on. "The thing is safe enough and won't capsize easily. She's nearly as broad as she's long and looks as if she'd stand up to almost anything. She's an old koster yacht, built on Koster Island on the west coast about fifty years ago."

"Oh," said Dessi, "I love kosters, there's such lovely oak in old kosters. And I've always liked a gaff rig."

"Until recently she belonged to the Canal Company in Södertälje and was used as a tugboat," Papa continued.

"But she really is a sailing boat?" I said.

"Yes, she was built as one. But she has an engine as well, an old oil-burning Bruzaholmer, with a hot-bulb ignition. The sails haven't been used for a long time. But they are in good condition. The mast is a bit on the short side, and she doesn't carry much canvas—about twenty square meters, I should say."

Twenty, I reflected. *Tanja III*, winner of many cups, was a yacht, carrying forty. A sailing koster has a heavy hull, and carrying so little canvas would certainly be incapable of much speed. There would assuredly be a big difference. I realized that. Papa read my thoughts.

"Yes, you must realize that she is no *Tanja III*," he said.

"Who wants a *Tanja III*?" I said. "This sounds like a splendid sailing boat. What's she called?"

"Guess!"

Now what would be a good name for a sailing koster, we wondered.

"What was that one in the Koster waltz called?" said Mama. "I know—Maja, like me. Is this one Maja, Patrik?"

"No, that she isn't," said Papa.

"Carmencita," suggested Mirre. "No? Well, how about Rosita?"

"That wouldn't be at all suitable for such a sturdy craft. Try again. And don't forget she must be fifty years old at least."

"Eleanor?" said Dessi. "Susannah? Esmeralda?"

"Flounder? Seagull? Frog?" said Knut and I.

"Albertina," said Mama.

"You're getting warm," said Papa. "But you haven't got it yet. I'd better tell you. She's called *Rudolfina*."

"Help!" said Knut.

"That sounds a bit nutty," said Mirre.

"There's no such name," I said.

"Perhaps the chap who built her was called Rudolf," said Dessi.

"And his sweetheart was Fina," said Mama.

"Well, anyway, we'll have to stick to that," said Rosalind. "It would be unlucky to change the name."

"What does the name matter?" I said. "We've got our very own boat, that's the chief thing."

"And the name is certainly unique," said Dessi.

"When you get accustomed to it, *Rudolfina*'s a great name," said Mirre.

"But where is this miracle, pray?" demanded Mama.

"*Rudolfina* is in dock for an overhaul, in Pershagen's yard just outside Södertälje. They'll sail her down in the middle of June just when we shall be moving out to the cottage."

"I wonder what the dye manager will think," said Knut.

CHAPTER TWO

RUDOLFINA ARRIVED. And then—well, who could resist her? Tubby and broad, her varnish a-gleam, she came chugging alongside Aunt Bella's jetty. She was as sturdy as an old market woman and her stout oaken hull looked capable of standing up to anything. She heeled over a bit, of course, when we all jumped on board at once, but there was nothing unstable about her. Even Mama ventured aboard, and she is a real landlubber.

"This boat isn't an elegant cockleshell like *Tanja III*," she said approvingly. "She's like a barge."

"Barge, indeed!" we shouted. "Our boat!" For now that *Rudolfina* was ours all other boats could go and sink themselves! Even *Tanja III*, which up to now we had regarded as the most wonderful craft in the world, had had her nose put out of joint.

Tanja III lay at anchor by her buoy, opposite the dye manager's house, looking very stately. But suddenly we felt she was too elegant and slender, which could not be said of our *Rudolfina*.

Tanja III was not merely a boat. She was a racing yacht and a real gem. At one time she had been our heaven, and all the summer we could talk of nothing but

Tanja this and *Tanja* that, using only seagoing terms in our conversation.

The manager's wife and son used at one time to go sailing with him. But the wife had gotten rheumatism and the son had gone to Australia just about the time that we came to live in Norrköping and spent our summers in Aunt Bella's cottage. The manager, who watched us rowing and swimming, was delighted to have new deckhands as close neighbors. He started teaching me sailing, but Rosalind gave him no peace until he let her come too. That made Dessi and Mirre wild. In the end I had to go as an ordinary hand every time, plus one of the girls, but they had to take turns because it didn't do to have more than three people aboard. Finally Knut sometimes came as well.

We were taught everything thoroughly and no mistake. The manager was the fussiest man I have ever met—aboard *Tanja III*, not otherwise. He was very nice at the same time, but he kept on until we knew how to do a thing inside out and could satisfy him in every particular. And though it may sound a bit boastful to say so, we soon learned practically everything that sailing folk ought to know.

We not only learned to read charts, but to know every shoal in Bråviken and the water round about, and how to make use of the tiniest little breeze, and how close inshore we could get before going about. We learned to listen for and obey commands in a flash. We learned to

clean and care for a boat exactly as a mother cat tends her babies, and even more so!

Every inch of *Tanja*'s dazzling deck was rubbed with chamois leather daily, her sheets were faultlessly coiled down. They looked like some elegant form of confectionery on a cake dish. When we lowered the sails and covered them, not a wrinkle was to be seen, and woe betide anyone who allowed the dinghy or one of the oars to touch the spotless planking for a single instant.

But perhaps it was just that very pernicketiness, as Knut called it the first time he went sailing in *Tanja*, that made us secretly tire a bit, at last, of being members of her crew. Mirre said once that it was probably why the manager's wife didn't want to go on sailing, and then Rosalind said that probably the son went to Australia because he had gotten sick of all the cleaning and polishing.

My only other unfavorable criticism of *Tanja* is that we could never all go aboard her at the same time, which was a great drawback as far as we were concerned. We were used to doing everything together, and the ones who had to be left ashore while the others were sailing used to feel peeved and discontented. You get like that when the sea fever really grips you.

But the Canal Company's old *Rudolfina* might have been built especially for us. We felt more at home right away on her scarred old deck than we ever had aboard *Tanja III*.

Papa came with us on our first trip, but only as a passenger. The dye manager inspected the boat and had a little jaunt in her and said she was reliable and homelike and easy. Later on he sat on his verandah, watching, as we brought her alongside the jetty, and gave us a word of advice from time to time. Otherwise we managed everything entirely by ourselves.

For my own part I had felt a bit uneasy for a moment when Mama was so taken with *Rudolfina*. I thought it meant we should always have our parents with us whenever we went sailing. Not that I have anything against them; they are both very decent. But there's nothing like going on a trip just with young people aboard. However, our parents understood that, so I needn't have worried.

For a week we went sailing every day. We sailed in Bråviken and really got to know our boat. She certainly was no racing yacht. There had to be a pretty stiff breeze before she got up anything like a good speed. At first we were inclined to think it beneath our dignity and felt it unseamanlike to set the engine going when the wind dropped, and we would lie waiting for hours a few hundred yards off the jetty. But presently we came down off our high horse and got out the blowlamp as soon as we felt things were getting too sluggish.

The old engine had a flywheel which had to be swung by hand when starting. It was under a cover in the well, and smoked a lot and smelled, especially when we had a following wind. But it was a good thing to have, anyhow.

Soon Bråviken became too confining for us. Rosalind and I had been as far as Sandhamn once, in *Tanja III*. Now we were longing to get out beyond the skerries again, this time on our own.

We invited Papa and Mama and Aunt Bella to a little sailing coffee party in the direction of Pampusfjärden, so that they could see how well we handled the boat. They highly approved of our seamanship and of *Rudolfina*, which was what we had intended. So when we all came in a body and begged to be allowed to make a real long trip, no one said no. I believe actually they were expecting it, though perhaps not quite so soon.

"Let them go," said the dye manager, and "Yes, Maja, let them go; they'll be all right," said Aunt Bella.

"Very well," said Mama, "but just let me finish the sleeping bags I am making out of old blankets."

Papa too said yes, but on certain conditions. I was certainly the one who knew most about sailing and managing the engine, but Dessi must be in charge, as she was the eldest, and we must always obey her. We were to have three proper meals a day, not just snacks and lemonade and that sort of thing. Our life belts must all be ready to hand in the well and never on any account stowed away or mislaid. All waste must be thrown out to sea well away from the shore. The blowlamp must be handled with the utmost caution, and both it and the primus stove must always be filled by the same careful person, Mirre, for instance. But after a lot of palaver I got him to agree to my being responsible for the blow-lamp, and Mirre for the primus.

We were to keep in touch with home by writing and telephoning whenever possible. The logbook must be strictly kept. Papa said that we must all help with it but that I was to do most of the writing, since I intended to be an author. No unnecessary risks must be taken. Night watches ought to be avoided. And we must stick together through thick and thin and not squabble too much.

We promised.

"How long may we go for?" we asked.

"Shall we say a month?" said Papa. "Will that suit you?"

"That's *quite* long enough," said Mama.

"Oooh!" was all we could say. A month! We had only dared hope for a week.

CHAPTER THREE

KNUT WAS THRILLED with the whole idea. "We'll cruise about and find some uninhabited islands where we can be absolutely on our own and arrange to barter things with the natives," he said.

Rosalind pointed out that in uninhabited islands there weren't any natives. But Knut said we would live on uninhabited islands and then go and descend on the inhabited ones and get to know the people there, of course.

Dessi said that for her part she thought it would be perfect to drop anchor by any convenient islet a long way out to sea, and stay there and sketch without people crowding around always staring.

"The archipelago is full of uninhabited islands," said Rosalind. "So we can single out the best and play Robinson Crusoe as much as we like. We can swim and build a hut of pine branches and make a raft while Dessi is painting."

I said that the most important thing was to find a good anchorage, sheltered from every wind, and they agreed with me. But Knut said we should be bound to meet a few storms and high winds occasionally or nothing exciting would happen.

"Hush! If Mama hears you she'll never let us go," we said.

Mirre wanted to make toward Möja, for that is where the best strawberries come from, she said, and she had always wanted to see the islands that were covered with them. Then we should be able to have as many as we wanted for once, since they were bound to be very cheap.

We studied the chart and found lots of enticing names that aroused our curiosity. Since we were to have no grownups with us we could go off course whenever we liked and go exploring around by Angödrommen and Bullerö and Lilla Nassa and all the rest.

It was Stockholm's outer archipelago that attracted us most.

"We'll sail just wherever we like," said Dessi. "I mean we won't bother to keep to any strict plan, because that's so dull. We'll just go where we please and stay just as long as we want to in each place."

"But suppose some of us want one place and some another?" I said.

"Obviously everyone will want the nicest place," said Mirre.

Pysen was determined to come with us. We said, "No, Pysen, nothing doing," but he wouldn't budge. He is awfully obstinate. When we began loading up with provisions and the other paraphernalia we needed, he came along, dragging his toys—the duck, and blocks, and motor cars called Fimbo and Lyxen. We took them all

back ashore, but no sooner had we done so than he brought them back again. And we carried them up and he carried them down, and so it went on.

"We men are going sailing with the girls," he said to Knut and me.

"Some other year," I said.

"You can go in the rowboat with Mama and Little O," said Knut.

"Oh noho, indeed I won't," he said, and trotted aboard again with Fimbo and Lyxen.

"I feel sorry for him," I said. "Little O is so young; he will be awfully lonely when we go."

"He'll bellow," said Dessi. "And the worst of it is that once he starts doing that he never leaves off. He'll howl every day until we get back."

"He doesn't bellow so often now," said Mama. "But it's quite true once he starts it's difficult to get him to stop. He sounds like a ship's siren. I can't think where the child got his voice from—it's like a trombone. Think what an advantage it would have been if I'd had one like that when I was on the stage ages ago. But you'll have to leave very early in the morning, before he's awake, then he'll realize nothing can be done about it."

"Say, you know," said Mirre, thoughtfully, "how about taking him with us after all? Why should he have to stay behind? It isn't fair."

Papa said that nobody who couldn't swim was to go on a long sailing trip.

"I can swim, oho yes," said Pysen, sticking his head out of the cabin. We were down by the jetty at the time.

"With a corkbelt on," said we. Because he had learned the strokes and did them very well for a four-year-old.

"How about making him wear a real life jacket the whole time?" said I.

"Do you really think you could look after him?" asked Mama.

"We always do look after him," said Mirre, who is the one who generally does so, as a matter of fact, or at least as much as I do.

"It wouldn't be any harder on board," said Dessi. "In fact it ought to be easier, actually. Nobody could fall into the water without the helmsman seeing him do so."

"We can tether him if he gets troublesome," said Rosalind.

"Let him come; it'll be all right," said I.

"It hardly seems wise; what do you think, Patrik?" said Mama.

"Well," said Papa, "I've got a hunch that he'll go, whatever our feelings may be on the subject. And if the youngsters really want him with them there's no good our objecting. So for my part I agree, on condition, of course, that you all promise to look after him."

We promised. But Knut said, "Oh, all right. But he's too young. And if he starts bellowing I shall go ashore."

"Silly Knut! I don't bellow, noho," said Pysen.

"There you are, isn't he intelligent!" said Mirre.

"If you start howling you'll go straight back home," I said.

"Well," said Mama, "I'll begin washing and ironing for him at once. It's a good thing it's such good drying weather. But how quiet and strange it will seem with only Little O at home. And I do wonder whether . . ."

"Don't start making objections now it's all settled," said I. "Pysen comes with us and that'll give you quite a little holiday, Mama. Won't that be nice?"

Pysen's eyes shone like two little Roman candles. Then he went ashore to fetch the duck and the building blocks for the fortieth time.

"He never had the slightest doubt about going," said Papa, gazing after his sturdy little figure.

"It would be no bad thing to be as self-confident as Pysen," murmured Dessi.

Dessi was sixteen and had never had any doubts regarding her intention of becoming an artist. Every now and then, however, she gets an attack of being unsure of herself and goes about hanging her head and saying her sketches don't amount to anything. The only way of bucking her up is by agreeing with her and saying yes, quite true, you draw like an old crow and your sketches look like nothing on earth. Then she starts defending them a bit, though she is never very satisfied with her own work and can't bear hearing it praised or knowing that we are proud of her.

There was no end to the gear we needed. We were going sailing for a whole month, if the weather stayed fine. *Rudolfina* was large and roomy. But all our woollies and warm clothes for chilly evenings, and the oilskins which the dye manager had given us, and provisions and water casks and Dessi's sketching material and my camera and all the hundred and one other items had to be stowed away. Half a sack of potatoes and fifteen packets of hard rye bread are pretty bulky in themselves, and a crate of lemonade and a carton of pots of jam take up a good deal of room as well.

"Anyway, Lars and Knut can start by sleeping in the tent," said Papa. "But there will be room on board after a while if you eat enough."

We said it would be quite O.K. sleeping in the tent.

We stowed and stowed, checking off each item against Papa's list. And at last we began to think we had everything. The last thing we took aboard was a Peep saucepan—how can anyone possibly go sailing without a Peep?

By five o'clock one sunny Sunday morning we were ready to set sail. We ate our early breakfast and drank our chocolate to the accompaniment of last admonitions from our (in spite of everything) rather worried parents.

It was obvious that Mama was worked up because of the way she went on talking without a single pause for punctuation, as she does when she is nervous.

"Keep a sharp lookout for adders and mind you buy milk whenever you can did I tell you I had put a pile of pillowcases in the middle locker Dessi are you positive that pump functions properly Patrik and don't stay too long in the water when you swim but come out before you turn blue and be good children and behave properly to Dessi because she is in charge of you all and have sensible meals and Lars you mustn't lie and read in bed who put the methylated spirits on board I wonder how many things we have forgotten toilet paper matches and kitchen paper we've put those in and you must take it in turns to wash up and peel potatoes and not go sneaking off and if you run aground let Pysen yell and someone will come and help you and if he . . . where is he?"

Pysen was never slow at putting in an appearance when food was around. We began looking for him.

"Who saw him last?"

"He was just outside the door, packing something into the basket he got yesterday," said Rosalind. "He's probably gone down to the boat with it."

She was quite right; there he was, clambering up onto the jetty. I've seldom seen a youngster as sure-footed as Pysen. He hardly ever falls down and hurts himself, though he patters all over the place.

"Don't you want anything to eat?" Mama asked him as he came in.

"Oho yes, indeed," said Pysen. He ate until he was

practically square. Then he got up and pulled my arm impatiently and said, "We must go now, come along."

But first we went to the paddock to say good-bye to Laban and Lotta who were grazing there. It seemed strange to Rosalind and me to think we shouldn't see them for a whole month, for we had groomed and fed them every winter and taken them out to grass every summer, and given them titbits of sugar, and understood what Lotta meant every time she pricked her constantly moving ears.

"I wish we could take them too," said Rosalind. "Good-bye, old Lotta. Good-bye, darling old Laban."

We were careful not to take them down to the shore, for Lotta, seahorse that she is, would certainly have come swimming after us as we sailed away.

CHAPTER FOUR

AT LAST we were all aboard. Mama hugged us and behaved as though she were never going to see us again. She hugged Pysen most, of course.

"Let me go," he said, struggling. "My life jacket hurts when you hug me. We men have got to hoist the sheets, yoho!" He meant the sails, of course. Knut and I were just hoisting the mainsail and he wanted to help and got in the way. It was going to be a nuisance, I thought. But when you've undertaken to look after a small boy you've just got to make the best of it.

Dessi, however, had a brainwave when she herself had finished hugging Little O, who, morning-fresh and bright-eyed, had come down to wave good-bye to us. Dessi is so fond of Little O that she had tried to persuade Mama to let her come along with us. It would have been a regular children's nursery, but Dessi wouldn't have minded a bit; she'd have liked it. The smaller children are the more she loves them.

"Pysen," she said, "as you've got the life jacket and everything, you must attend to the flag. Remember you'll have to fetch it and unroll it and stick the handle in this hole in the stern, here, every morning. Like this—see?

Do it now, to see if you can. Mind it doesn't fall into the sea. There, that was fine! Now you are the flag officer aboard. No one but you must hoist the flag and you must do it as soon as you wake up in the morning."

Pysen was very proud. He realized that his was a responsible post.

"It's my flag, yoho!" he said. "I'm the flagsiffer!"

Rosalind cast off and Dessi took the tiller. Papa and Mama jumped ashore with Little O and stood on the jetty, with many anxious parental wrinkles in their foreheads. Aunt Bella, who was down there too, gave the bow a shove with her sturdy foot and Rosalind drew in the fenders and saw to the dinghy.

"Good-bye, children, enjoy yourselves!" cried Aunt Bella. "You've got a glorious day."

"Bye-bye, silden," piped Little O, laughing so that the dimples showed in her cheeks.

Knut and I hoisted the sails, the mainsail first and then the foresail. There wasn't much wind as yet, just a faint little morning breeze. We glided out along the shore, then headed eastward.

"Hurrah!" we all shouted. "Good-bye, good-bye!"

"Call us whenever you can get to a telephone," called Mama.

"Trim the sails, Rosalind," ordered Dessi. "Look out for the boom. Mirre, the gulls have left their card on deck, you'll have to scrub it—Pysen, get the mop and give it to Mirre, yes, that's the one. Knut, those lashings mustn't be left on the deck."

"Aye aye, Captain," said Knut, stowing away the lashings while Mirre scrubbed.

"What shall I do now?" asked the flag officer, gazing around.

"Wave nicely to Papa and Mama and Little O and Aunt Bella, because the rest of us haven't time just at the moment," I said. "And then you must watch and see that

none of us gets in the way of this dangerous great boom."

"Dangerous big boom boom," said Pysen.

"Because it swings around awfully quickly and could knock us into the sea if we weren't careful. You shall be the lookout, and stay down there in the well, because that's the best place to watch it from. And when it swings you must shout 'Look out!' as hard as you can so that we can dodge it."

Pysen waved dutifully for half a minute to those left behind on the jetty. Then he took up his position on the seat, gazing threateningly and eagerly up at the boom. We glided past *Tanja III*, lying moored to her buoy, slim as a tern. A handkerchief fluttered from the dye manager's bedroom window, and we waved back.

"Poor man, he must wish he were with us," said Rosalind.

"We'll go about now," said Dessi. "All ready?"

"Here comes the dreadful boom boom," shrieked Pysen. "Take care, everybody!"

" 'Look out!' is what you have to say," I told him.

"Noho," he replied, "I shall say dreadful big boom boom."

The sun shone, the water glittered, the breeze blew caressingly, the shore slipped by, green and leafy. Nobody spoke for a little while. Right down in all our hearts was a special sort of feeling that we were perfectly free. This was no little coffee picnic. A whole month at sea, a whole month without our parents or any guardian or yachting experts. No school, no lessons, no set times for anything.

"Lars," said Dessi, looking rather strange, "be a dear and take the tiller for a bit."

"Aye aye, Captain," I said, going over to her on the double. "What's up? You don't feel ill or anything, do you?"

"No," she answered. "But I'm so happy I'm afraid of running us aground. I must pull myself together a bit before I dare go on steering."

I knew just how she felt. She lay on her back on the foredeck, gazing up at the sky and the white sails against the blue.

Mirre went down into the cabin to stow away the last gear we had brought aboard. Pysen gazed anxiously after her.

"You mustn't touch my things, oh noho," he cried.

"I won't even look at them," she called back from inside. "I'm only going to tidy up a little. Say, what's in this briefcase?"

"Don't go meddling with that; it's mine," cried Knut. "I got it from Papa."

"For goodness' sake," muttered Mirre, "how fussy men are over their toys."

"Toys, indeed," said Knut. "One isn't a baby, thank you all the same."

Knut had given up playing with model airplanes. He collected pretty stones and stamps instead. And he read heaps of books about explorers and pirates. We all read a

lot except Mirre. She is by way of being the practical one.

I gazed around. Aunt Bella's jetty was no bigger than a cigarette carton now, and the waving figures were like toy soldiers. I waved back for a bit and never noticed that I was sailing too close to the wind and that the sail was shaking.

"Hey, Lars!" shouted Rosalind as the boom swung. "That was bad! You know the manager must be watching us through his telescope."

"Dreadful big boom boom, watch everybody!" called Pysen.

"That's right, Pysen," I said. "You are much more careful than I am, though you were a bit late about it."

"I don't like that old boom boom," said he. "I shall go in and play."

"Go along, then," I said. As long as he was playing with Fimbo and Lyxen we knew he was quite safe.

Perfect weather and a gentle breeze—we couldn't have wished for a better start. But Knut said, "I wish the wind were a bit stronger; we're making practically no headway. Look at that swanky yacht skimming along."

"Well, she's carrying at least three times as much sail," said I.

"Throw a coin over the sail, Knut, then you'll get a favorable wind," said Rosalind, giving me a wink. Because Knut is the businessman of the family and not at all the sort of boy to throw his money into the sea. But wonders will never cease; he fished a coin out of his pocket and began taking aim.

"You'd better let Lars throw it," said Rosalind, "he's a better shot." Knut handed me the coin. It was a Norwegian two-öre piece. We've got lots of them at home; I don't know where they came from. You aren't allowed to use them when paying for things. Knut is practical. He thinks everything will come in handy sometime.

"Blow, Kajsa!" I cried and flung up the coin. It flew in a magnificent arc over the rigging and fell into the water a long way off. Knut gazed after it.

"We'll get a breeze now," he said delightedly. "It will be nice to get away from this little puddle. And if that one isn't enough, I've got plenty more in my pocket."

The "puddle" was Bråviken. Knut had been to a summer camp by the Åland Sea, and such gentlemen have not much time for Bråviken, however pleasant it may prove as a place to swim in.

"We forgot to say good-bye to Persson," said Rosalind as she lay sunning herself on deck.

Persson is Aunt Bella's cat. It's a she-cat, but it's always called Persson. I have explained this before, of course, but I had better do so once more for safety's sake, because Persson is rather an important character in this book.

"Miaow!" sounded at that very moment.

At first I thought Persson had hidden herself somewhere on board and was answering when she heard her own name. But then I remembered Knut. He was sitting there looking far too innocent.

"You're improving," I said to him. His highest ambition at that time was to become a ventriloquist, but he hadn't yet quite caught the trick. He used to practice imitating Persson and Miss Lur's cock without opening his mouth.

"What?" he said. "That wasn't me; it sounded exactly like Persson."

"Don't try that one," I replied. "It won't take us in; it wasn't as good as all that."

"Miaow!" sounded again. "*Miaow!*"

"You did that really well," said Rosalind. "It sounded exactly as though it were coming from somewhere down there." She pointed down into the well. Knut was lying on the cabin roof.

"But it wasn't me, I tell you," he repeated. "Don't you hear what I say?"

"Miaow!" It sounded most plaintive, just like Persson when she has been shut out and wants to come in.

"Yes, it did absolutely," I agreed. "It was better that time. I never thought you'd learn the trick, but now you are a real ventriloquist. You'll be able to earn money at it. Was that what you meant when you kept babbling about doing good business on this trip?"

But Knut jumped down onto the deck. "Either the cat is aboard or Mirre is playing a trick on us," he said, sticking his head in the cabin. "Was that you mewing, Mirre?"

"What are you burbling about?" said Mirre from inside. "Pysen is playing in the fo'c'sle and I'm putting things to rights. Nobody is mewing."

"Miaow! *Miaow!* MIAOW!"

"It *is* Persson; it must be," I said. "Persson, where are

you? Come along!" Pysen came climbing up out of the cabin.

"Persson, darling little Persson," he called coaxingly.

"Pysen!" I said. "Did you see if the cat smuggled herself on board?"

"Noho!" said Pysen, nodding with satisfaction. "I brought her."

"My goodness, whoever heard the like?" exclaimed Rosalind. "Dessi, just come and listen to this. The child's brought the cat aboard."

"Gracious me, what an idea," said Dessi. "Where did you put it, Pysen?"

"In the kennel," said Pysen, laughing delightedly.

"What kennel?" I asked. But then I understood. Under the hood covering the engine! It was not unlike the old kennel in Miss Lur's garden.

"Take the tiller, somebody," I said. Dessi took it. I raised the top of the cover. There was a basket inside. In the basket sat Persson, round and gray, blinking at the sunshine with brilliant golden eyes. "Miaow!" she said.

The next moment she escaped from her prison, leapt out, and began promenading around the deck.

"Now, Pysen," said Dessi, trying not to burst out laughing, as were we all, "why did you put the cat under the engine hood?"

"There's no dog," said Pysen solemnly. "Persson was playing at being a dog in the kennel."

"Well, well," said Mirre, "now we've got a ship's cat to look after as well."

"A stowaway," I said.

"But what will Aunt Bella say?" asked Rosalind. "We'll have to turn back and take Persson ashore."

"Noho!" shrieked Pysen.

Knut said it was an absolutely rotten idea. Were we going to have to keep dawdling around old Bråviken the whole time and never get any farther? Then the cat, having finished her tour of inspection of the cabin and fo'c'sle, came trotting up to Pysen and rubbed herself against him, purring.

"No, what's the good of putting the cat ashore?" said Mirre. "It just wants to be with Pysen. Think how bored it would be without him at home."

"If you're so keen on going back we'd better put Pysen ashore as well," muttered Knut. "The whole silly business is his fault."

But Dessi said, "Keep calm, everyone; here comes a steamer and we shall get the wash."

On she came, big and white and full of people who all waved and laughed when they had to make way for *Rudolfina*. And when she had passed us and we had tossed up and down a bit, Dessi continued. "I don't think we'll turn back. We'll phone from somewhere and tell them all about it so that Aunt Bella won't be worried about the cat, and then we'll keep her aboard, of course."

"But supposing she runs away sometime when we go ashore," I said. "Aunt Bella wouldn't be very pleased with us about that."

"Persson doesn't run away; she's just like a dog," said Rosalind. "We'll look after her. I'll catch fish for her."

"No, I will," said Knut, now no longer at all put out.
He enjoyed fishing and had learned how to do it that
summer by the Åland Sea. Then we discussed whether to
anchor and have lunch and then swim. But we decided to
go on sailing and have our meal while doing so. Rosalind
scrubbed potatoes, and Mirre lit the spirit stove and we
heated up Mama's hamburgers and ate our fill and
drank all the milk we wanted.

Then Pysen took Persson in his arms and carried her
down into the cabin with Fimbo and Lyxen and the
duck. And they went to sleep for three hours, Pysen still
wearing his life jacket and Persson purring sweet lull-
abies.

CHAPTER FIVE

BY THE TIME we had washed up, the wind had died down so that the sails hung like window curtains. The Norwegian coin hadn't accomplished much. Knut said there was a cloud bank to the northwest and that it might mean the wind was getting up, but he didn't really believe this himself. Dessi and I studied the chart and held a consultation. We had come only a little way past Nävekvarn. Should we be satisfied with that and go in search of an anchorage for the night behind the islands there? We'd feel rather foolish not to have done more during the whole of the first day, for we had expected to be decidedly farther north.

"Couldn't we start up the engine so as to get on just a little?" I said. We couldn't pretend, of course, that we were in any hurry. But it was a good old engine, and truth to tell I wanted to show them how well I managed it. Besides, the dye manager had said, "Oh, yes, they may think themselves lucky if they get as far as Nävekvarn the first day, in that boat." It annoyed us that he should prove to be right.

The open sea lay before us, and though not quite as calm as a mill pond, it was nearly so. We saw one or two other sailing boats, big modern yachts, and though they weren't exactly going fast, they were all obviously doing better than we were with our light rig. But we were eager to have *Rudolfina* make good speed, so I fetched the blowlamp and started warming up the hot bulb. It took a little time. Knut and Rosalind watched admiringly as I swung the great flywheel and the first spluttering throbs were heard. *Rudolfina* didn't sound a bit like the usual sort of motorboat, and she wasn't, either. There were such long pauses between the explosions. She didn't rattle but made a noise like stonka stonka stonka, very high and clear and with a little echo after each stonka. We left a dark smoke track and a pretty strong smell in our wake.

When we chuffed past a yacht of the six-meter class, nearly as slim and shining as *Tanja III*, we noticed the people laughing at us, but we didn't care.

"Swanky crowd," said Knut again.

The summer before, he had been absolutely crazy about sailing aboard *Tanja III*, and she was even swankier than this particular boat. But we understood his feelings and shared them. We all preferred *Rudolfina*. No other boat was a patch on her.

"Listen!" I yelled at our crew so as to make myself heard above the noise of the stonka stonka. "We'll go to Sandhamn sometime this summer and show them all what a boat ought to look like."

"Yes! Let's," they yelled back. "We'll go to the regatta."

Then we waved a proud farewell to the six-meter boat.

"Perhaps we ought to have asked if we could give them a tow," said Rosalind. "Because, after all, Rudolfina is an old tugboat."

"Well, is there anything wrong in that?" demanded Knut pugnaciously.

"Wrong?" said Rosalind. "Why, it would be simply marvelous if we could tow a boat like that when she could make no headway."

"Shall we go about and ask them?" I said. "We might be the ones to need help another time." The dye manager had taught us this.

Dessi put the helm hard over. We went about and stonka'd round the six-meter in a wide circle. She lay motionless, becalmed, the wind having dropped. I called across.

"Hullo, there! If you'd like a tow, throw us a line."

We couldn't hear what they said in reply and had to stop the engine and ask them to repeat it.

"We said thanks very much, but we don't want to be killed by fumes from that old stinkadora. We'd rather wait for the evening breeze."

"If we had a cannon on board I should shoot them," said Knut. "Stinkadora, indeed!"

"Well, crude oil does stink a bit, you can't get away from that," said Dessi. But I called back to the yacht, "You've only yourselves to blame." And I started up the engine once more.

Presently Mirre said, "We are funny, when you come to think of it. Last year, when Lars and I were deckhands on *Tanja III*, we used to laugh sometimes at old boats like this with their oil-burning engines. 'Look at that scruffy old thing,' we used to say."

"Yes, but *Rudolfina* wasn't one of them—and she isn't scruffy," I said.

We puttered on. The sun shone and the deck planking burned our bare feet. Now and then a puff of wind played with the sail, but that was all. Rosalind lay on her back, reading *National Velvet* by Enid Bagnold. It is her favorite book and she takes it with her wherever she goes. Knut leaned against the mast, reveling in a pirate story. As he read he kept wobbling a loose tooth. He was going to pull it out himself when he felt like doing so, he said, and didn't need to go to a dentist. When we had bread and butter he would only eat the soft part of the bread and chewed on one side of his mouth. Pysen crawled around in the cockpit, having races with Fimbo and Lyxen, watched by Mirre, as she sat marking towels with "Rudolfina" in blue cross-stitch. Dessi sat forward with Persson on her lap. The foresail hid her from me where I sat at the tiller, but that she was still happy was a pretty sure guess. Persson was settling down well to being a ship's cat, but avoided going too close to the stonka-engine. She watched the gulls that followed us and a big bumblebee that had come all the way from home with us and kept banging itself against us and the sails, obviously bemused and dizzy.

The afternoon went by and I began searching the chart for a good anchorage for the night. I found one some way east of Oxelösund which I thought suitable. It was a curved bay, with a tongue of land running southward out toward the sea approach. We should be well sheltered there, I thought, and I pointed it out to Knut.

"Not bad," he said approvingly. "It looks just like a lagoon, with a coral reef and everything."

It took a little time to reach it. The sun had begun to set by the time we got there, and the bay looked somewhat dark and sullen, but otherwise all right. The cliffs were rather high, and what I had taken for a flat headland proved to be a steep one. Such things aren't shown on a chart. But it was all the better for *Rudolfina*—it would do splendidly for her.

"This is a good harbor," I said. "If we put in just alongside this headland we shall be sheltered from the east wind if it begins to blow." The girls agreed. So we dropped anchor in the lee of the headland.

While the girls prepared a meal, Knut and I went ashore in the dinghy to put up the tent. Pysen and Persson came too, for you could see that Persson wanted to scratch around a bit.

It was rock everywhere, but we managed to find a fairly good spot for the tent in a cleft a bit inland. Pysen helped by handing us tent pegs, and before we had even gotten the canvas fixed and everything taut and shipshape, he crawled inside and said, "We men will sleep here. Persson as well."

"Noho, you and Persson will sleep on board," said Knut.

"I shall sleep here, yoho," said Pysen and stayed put.

"Aha!" said I. "Then Rosalind will hoist the flag tomorrow. She will enjoy that. And the sun will soon have gone down, so she will haul down the flag too if you don't look sharp."

Then he remembered he was the flag officer and had his duties to perform, so he stopped being a nuisance and agreed to return at once. The girls called that the food was ready, and we rowed out to Rudolfina, and Pysen hauled down the flag. Then we ate pork and macaroni until we nearly burst. We sat in the cabin as we ate, for it had suddenly grown rather chilly. Even Rosalind noticed it and she is a person who never feels the cold. She had had a dip before the meal and she said the water felt unusually wet, like when one swims in November. Rudolfina swayed a little, uneasily, for it was beginning to blow a bit.

"Can you manage all right alone, girls?" I asked when we had washed up. Pysen was already tucked in with Persson and the duck, and we others were yawning, for we had started the day unusually early. The girls said "yes." None of them wanted to go ashore before next morning, they said, so we could take ourselves off in the dinghy with a clear conscience. And if anything happened, they could always shout. So Knut and I collected our gear and headed for the shore.

First we went a little way up the rock. The sky looked

so queer, now that the sun had disappeared. A sort of ominous brassy yellow and black. And the clouds were like great gray elephants. Out to sea the waves were quite high, dark green with crests.

"Getting breezy," I said to Knut as we stood fighting with the wind.

"I knew there would be wind," he said, "but it might have come a bit sooner."

"You mean because of the Norwegian coin?" said I.

"Pooh!" he replied, but added presently, "One never knows." Then we went to turn in. He had brought the big briefcase with him from the boat. It was an old one of Papa's that he had had when he was a commercial traveler.

"What on earth have you got that for?" I asked.

"Well, the girls might have gone rummaging about in it," he said.

"They wouldn't. And anyway, is there anything so terribly private inside?"

"I'll show you," he said.

"Now? This minute?"

"Well, I don't know." He hesitated. "All right, then, if you promise to hold your tongue."

"O.K.," I said. "Come on, then, and let's see."

He looked very serious. I lay there shining the flashlight as he opened the briefcase and began taking things out of it.

Then I sat up and stared. Little pocket mirrors, small red and blue combs, a few rings and brooches with flash-

ing stones, some pink soap, a penknife, three little cel-
luloid ducks, some folders with envelopes and writing
paper and a number of little green gauze bags full of
beads, obviously bought from a cheap store in the
town.

"Do . . . are you thinking of going around selling that
stuff?" I asked.

He nodded. "I've spent almost all my pocket money on
it," he said, "but I expect to make a good profit."

"Do you really believe they'll want such rubbish out in
the archipelago?" I said.

"Of course," he replied. "They couldn't get things like
this on the islands, you see. I could exchange them, too,
for food, or other things we might need. Dessi could pay
me out of the housekeeping purse instead. I mean, supposing we wanted milk. I could exchange it for a little
comb or looking glass, and Dessi could give me what the
milk would have cost, and that sort of thing."

"You wouldn't get much milk for one of those," I said,
looking at one of the trashy little combs.

"We'll see," returned Knut, compressing his lips.

"And the beads. Who do you think would want
them?"

"Oh, people who live on remote islands always like
beads."

"But what would they use them for?" I asked, trying to
keep as serious as possible, though I was bursting with
laughter inside.

"Well, I don't know exactly; necklaces and that sort of

thing, and . . . well, it's almost as good as money in some parts, you know. And they like bright-colored cotton stuff, too, but I couldn't afford any."

Knut had read a great deal about exploring expeditions in South America and the South Sea Islands in olden days.

"When you were by the Åland Sea with the summer colony that time," I said, "did they want beads and that sort of thing there?"

"Poof! There were only helpers and matrons besides us, and anyway I was only seven then and didn't think about such things."

"Well, I don't think much of the idea," I said.

"Of course, you don't, you never do believe in my ideas, any of you," said Knut huffily.

"Look here, don't take it like that," I said. "All I meant was—"

"I know exactly what you meant," said Knut. "But I'll show you and the others, too, so there!"

Knut isn't like the rest of us. It's not just that he is so keen on making a bargain, but he's so touchy and sometimes as prickly as a hedgehog. I can't always make him out. He's more than three years younger than me and has always been on his own rather a lot. I've generally gone about more with Rosalind. She's just a year older than me and almost like a boy, and we have fun together. Of course Knut's often been with us as well, but perhaps not as often as he'd have liked.

He packed the things back into the briefcase and fastened it securely. Then we put out the light. Outside, the wind blew and tore at the tent so that one felt it might be swept away.

"There's going to be a storm," I said uneasily.

"Yes," murmured Knut sleepily, "but you've only yourself to blame. Didn't you order the wind to blow?"

"Oh, nonsense," I said. "But I wonder how *Rudolfina* will weather a storm in this cove."

"You said she'd be sheltered from the wind all around."

"Yes, I *think* she'll be all right, but one can never be certain. Perhaps we oughtn't to have left the girls all on their own."

I lay listening for a time. Yes, it really was blowing up for a real storm—there was no doubt about that.

CHAPTER SIX

I FELT I MUST get up and have a look at our boat. I wriggled out of my sleeping bag and opened the zip fastening of the tent. Whew! The wind rushed in through the flap and filled the whole tent, blowing it up like a balloon. We had pitched it with the opening toward the sea, not having expected anything of this sort. Now the wind had turned easterly and we got the full force of the gale. The noise and fury outside were continuous and my thin pajamas filled like a sail, and gave about as much warmth. It was extraordinary that it should be so cold in summer.

I climbed out of the cleft and peered toward the point. At first I couldn't distinguish anything. Then I made out something I took to be *Rudolfina*. How odd! She had grown larger. She loomed through the darkness like a great heaving gray mass. Why, what was that? She was no longer at anchor; she was coming nearer, her engine was going! Stonka stonka stonka could be heard even above the noise of the storm. How had the girls started the engine? They had never before attempted to do so. And why? Why start up the engine when the boat lay at anchor? Had she dragged her moorings?

I started to run, scrambling over the rocks, tripped over a juniper bush and fell headlong. But I saw that *Rudolfina* still lay at anchor in the lee of the headland, safe and sound. The stonka stonka came from another, much bigger boat, making her way into the cove in search of shelter for the night. Ah! Now they had caught sight of *Rudolfina*. The best anchorage was taken—what a bit of bad luck! They went about, evidently intending to move off again. A sailing boat—no, not a sailing boat. She had no mast, or only a little stump as far as I could see. But she had been sailing, all the same. That is to say a huge sail had been torn and was fluttering and thrashing all over the place. There! Now it had blown into the water! At the same instant a whole swarm of big white— could it be birds?—flew up. They must be birds, for they were so light and spread out all over the cove, alighting on the water and floating like swans.

I thought I must be dreaming. A big sailing boat without a mast, and with a cargo of white birds! What a weird ghost ship!

But now the engine stopped and I heard the rattle of chains. The anchor was being dropped. I had to get closer and see more of this. I groped my way down to the shore. Just as my bare feet touched the outermost rocks, one of the swans came flying right past my face, brushing my nose before falling into the water. And now I saw it was no swan, not a bird at all, but a basket, an ordinary basket, with a handle and everything. The whole cove was full of baskets tossing in toward the land.

I reached out and got hold of the basket. Before me lay the peculiar boat. Now that she was securely anchored they were trying to rescue the sail that had gone into the water. It was easier said than done, a wet sail is extremely heavy and there were evidently only two men on board.

"Ahoy!" I hailed them, putting up my hands to form a megaphone. "Shall I come and help?"

"Come on," shouted someone in reply. "Have you got a boat there?"

I went to the dinghy—yes, it was still there. I pushed her out, but the sea drove her back time after time. At last I gave up.

"I can't launch her," I yelled. "I'll try and save the baskets instead." For now they had blown together in a great drift at the head of the bay not far from our camping place. I ran back to the tent and roused Knut.

"Get up and come and help," I cried. He got up, shivering and half awake, and I explained as we ran. He said nothing but ran for dear life. Then we gathered baskets from land and sea. Little ones and big ones, round ones and oblong ones—I've never seen so many baskets in all my life. First we piled them on the beach, but the wind blew the pile away, scattering them all over the place. Then we carried them up to the tent and put them in there. When one is carrying a great armful of baskets one is practically windborne. We were blown across the rocks and into the tent without any effort.

"I'm flying!" screamed Knut. "Did you see?"

Aboard the strange boat they had managed at last to salvage the sail. Now a dinghy put off and came toward us. An old chap jumped ashore. He had a pipe in one corner of his mouth and an old yachting cap which seemed glued to his head.

"That was decent of you youngsters," he said. And then he started collecting baskets as well. We had to wade in waist deep or even further to get some of them and it was quite a time before we had collected them all. It looked awfully funny to see the old chap scrambling about in the sea with all his clothes on and his pipe in his mouth. We were just about frozen stiff when it was all over and there were no more "swans" to be seen in the water. Then we found a whole lot tangled up in the brambles and wild roses. But the tent was too full to hold any more, so we put them in a crevice of the rock face, laying a stone in each. We scared a lot of sea birds when we went up there, and they shrieked and fluttered, and the sea thundered and there was a tremendous din.

Then, from the sea, we heard a cry of distress.

"Kalle! Kalle! *Dunkan*'s dragging. Come quick!"

The old chap didn't say a word or take the pipe out of his mouth. He simply went down to the sea and pushed out his dinghy, which incidentally wasn't a real dinghy but an old barge punt. We followed.

"Can we help anymore?"

"Come aboard or you'll freeze to death," he said.

"Pooh, the water was quite warm," I said as we took our places in the punt.

"The air is cold and your tent's full of baskets, and who

knows if I could fetch you, later on, now it's blowing like this."

The trip to the boat wasn't easy; it took all his strength, and a dinghy wouldn't have made it, but a punt moves more lightly and easily over the water. The waves dashed spray over me where I sat in the bow, but as I was already wet through it didn't matter.

"What a lovely rough sea!" said Knut, enraptured.

I don't know how we got aboard—he threw us up as if we were a pair of gloves or something—and the person who had screamed caught us as we tumbled on deck.

"I thought it was blowing great guns, but now I see it has blown small boys tonight," she said. "And what's become of Kalle?"

"I'm coming," said Kalle.

The boat was a full-decked barge, dating apparently from the Ark. In the stern was quite a little house with a tinplate smoke stack, and behind that was a cockpit where the engine was, one like ours but bigger. The rest of the boat was obviously a cargo hold. Roughly folded and hurriedly thrust down into the cockpit was what I had taken for a sail. It was a big tarpaulin that had been used to cover the baskets, which had formed the deck cargo—the swans that went overboard when the wind blew aside the tarpaulins. Kalle took stock of the barge's situation.

"Drat it if she isn't going to drag her anchor," he said. "I'll have to have a go at that blessed engine. It takes time, but we'll see if we can manage it. I think I'll put out another anchor first." He disappeared for'ard.

"If it's an old Bruzaholmer, perhaps I can get it going," I said to the old woman. "Where's the blowlamp? Ah, here it is. And the matches?"

She gave me the matches and I knelt down and went through the lengthy performance with starting that I was used to in *Rudolfina*. I heard the anchor splashing for-'ard. The boat rolled and creaked and crackled. Only after some time did I realize that it was the cargo of baskets making the noise. Knut stood beside me, his teeth chattering, staggering from time to time but keeping firm hold of the tiller, which was as long as a boom.

"Are we going aground?" I asked as Kalle came running back. He didn't answer but looked anxious.

"Ah, good lad, you're warming her up, that's fine," he said. "We'll have to try and run in alongside the headland, but it's a narrow approach. I generally anchor over yonder, but now that other contraption's been and got there first. In this wind there's no sheltered spot in the cove except in the lee of that headland."

"That's our koster lying there," I said.

"And you leave her in weather like this?"

We said we had a brother and sisters aboard, and that there wasn't room for all of us to sleep comfortably, and he quite understood.

"But you're soaked to the skin, laddies," said the old woman. "Into the cabin with you and get some dry clothes on."

We pretended not to hear. We simply couldn't go away just when it was so exciting. Kalle hung over the afterdeck, watching the anchor chain.

"I think we're still dragging," he said.

"We're being driven ashore," said the old woman. And we saw that we were being brought closer to the cliff with every wave.

"The hot bulb's beginning to get red—we'll have her started soon," I said.

"No good hurrying," warned Kalle. "She'll only act up."

A big sea broke against the hull and the boat wallowed like a rocking chair.

"Now!" said Kalle and I with one voice, and he began swinging the flywheel. But the engine wouldn't fire.

"You cantankerous lazybones!" said Kalle to the engine. "Are you going to let me down and get us beached, drat you? Where are your manners?"

He tried again and yet again. The whole time he had the empty pipe in the corner of his mouth. The third time the engine started up. Pysh, pysh, stonka stonka! What a welcome sound!

"Here, take the tiller, Vendla," he said hastily. "And you," he said to me, "go ahead slowly until I've got up the port anchor. Then we'll coax up the other as quick as blazes and go full steam ahead. You, Vendla, keep to the right of that pine tree there until I come and take over."

Vendla and I did exactly as we were told, or so we thought. It was heavy work for Kalle, getting the anchor up. Knut tried to help him but was shouldered aside. Kalle had one anchor up and the other hanging halfway when he shouted and came rushing astern again, brandishing his arms.

"Look out for the koster for the love of Mike," he yelled, snatching the tiller from the old woman. "You were steering straight for the koster. I know I said make for the lee of the headland, but not so as to collide with her!"

We succeeded in getting in to shelter behind *Rudolfina*, and came safely to rest. It was a narrow shave because of the way we were tossing, and was a dangerous maneuver, not to be undertaken lightly, but it turned out all right.

"Look, there are the girls," said Knut, his teeth chattering. We were so close to *Rudolfina* now that we could clearly see three figures watching us.

"Hi there!" cried Knut and I. "Are you O.K.?"

Dessi answered something we couldn't catch. Mirre tried again, and then it went better. "We've got the coffeepot going!" she called, "And hot milk, too. Come over, all of you!"

"Coffee!" said Vendla. "That sounds good. What do you say, Kalle?"

"Just the thing," he replied. "But first I'll drop the port anchor and put on a pair of dry trousers. Then we'll have to do a bit of pumping, for we've shipped a lot of water."

We helped pump. Then we paddled over in the punt. This trip was considerably smoother than the other one.

The girls had bathrobes on over their nightgowns and weren't as chilled as we were. Knut and I were almost overwhelmed by Mirre, who practically tore us to bits and thrust masses of woollies and oilskins upon us so that we shouldn't catch cold. It was good to get out of our soaking pajamas. Then we squeezed into the cabin, where the kerosene lamp was burning and Pysen and Persson lay asleep in a corner.

"That's a nice little shaver there," said Kalle, looking at Pysen. "A sturdy youngster, that."

"And you children are all on your own, sailing around in this beautiful cutter?" said Kalle's wife, looking as if she thought old Rudolfina's newly painted cabin was the last word in elegance.

"Yes," we said, "and we hope to have a whole month of it."

"You're like me," said Kalle, "there's nothing like the sea. Well, I reckon we should introduce ourselves. My name is Kalle Hamberg, though everyone calls me Kalle Hamper, and you can too. My old woman's called Vendla, and we're from Mistermåla."

"Where is that?" asked Mirre.

"In Småland, of course," said Kalle. "The cleverest and shrewdest folk all live in Småland, though I says it myself."

"Don't blow your own trumpet," said Vendla, laughing. She stuck a sugar lump between her teeth and sucked her coffee through it.

"Why not?" said Kalle, and at last filled and lit his pipe. "Thank you for the coffee. It was nice and hot and it's wrapped itself round my innards like cotton wool."

"Yes, it was lovely," said Vendla. "Just what we needed. And buns, too!"

"Just think, for once she agrees with me!" said Kalle
Hamper. Vendla laughed. Her round face was full of
cheerful little wrinkles when she did so.

"Don't you believe him," she said. "Nobody says 'yes'
and 'amen' more easily than I do."

We sat there a long time, drinking coffee and hot milk
and telling each other all about ourselves. We learned
that Kalle had gone to sea in his youth, but that now he

had a basket- and brush-making business with his two brothers. They usually sold their goods in the country inland, but every summer Kalle made a trip to Västervik where he kept the boat. Then he went on a cruise along the coast with *Dunkan,* as the boat was called, selling baskets and brushes and carpet beaters and wicker chairs out in the archipelago to people and to the summer visitors, as he put it. He had to do this, he said, or he would have gone to sea for good. But after his little summer trips he was contented and willing to stay at home making baskets till the following summer. Sometimes he went south—he had stonka'd away as far as Blekinge with his baskets. But otherwise he preferred Stockholm's outer archipelago and was on his way there, like us. He sold his goods really well there, he said. Vendla nodded. Kalle went out to see to *Dunkan.*

"Oh, I do think he's nice!" said Mirre. "It must be wonderful being married to such an interesting man."

"Yes," said Vendla, looking pleased. "He is kind and good as well. He has his faults, of course, but then we all have, so I mustn't grumble."

"What sort of faults?" demanded Knut inquisitively, but Dessi shut him up. Kalle came striding back.

"Rough weather still," he said, "but *Dunkan's* lying as snug as in an English iron bedstead. And now we must say thank you and take ourselves off, Vendla, so that these here little 'uns can get turned in. They are yawning fit to swallow a horse and cart."

"We aren't a bit sleepy," we assured him. "We'd

much sooner hear about how you went sailing in *Dunkan*, Uncle Kalle."

"Say Kalle and Vendla, as I told you. No, it won't do to sit up any longer; do you know it's almost half past twelve? But how will you manage, boys? You'd better come with us and doss down aboard *Dunkan*, for we've more room in her."

"Thank you, but we can manage all right here just for one night," we said.

"I'll lie on the cabin floor," said Rosalind, "and Lars can have my bunk in the fo'c'sle and Knut can lie on the sail bag."

"Just as you like," said Kalle. "And sleep sound, every-one, for I'll look after *Rudolfina* and *Dunkan*. I shall sleep with one eye open on a night like this."

"And tomorrow I invite you all to breakfast," said Vendla. "Kalle shall come and fetch you, for your own little dinghy is ashore."

"What time?" we asked.

"Oh, we'll take things easy after such a late night. We'll eat when we all wake up, not before! Kalle and I left Västervik at four o'clock this morning, so we shan't be up very early tomorrow, either. Thank you all, and good night."

"And thanks for helping with the baskets," said Kalle as he jumped into the punt and handed Vendla down.

We stood in the stern and watched them until they were safely back in the barge again. Then we tumbled into bed. For my part I was yawning until my jaw cracked. Knut wriggled about on the sail bag at my elbow.

"What do you think Vendla meant about Kalle having faults?" he asked.

"No idea," I replied.

"But what do you think?"

"Perhaps he's too sharp a businessman," I said.

"Don't talk nonsense," said Knut.

Then he fidgeted again.

"Lie still and go to sleep," I said.

"How can I, with my head down and my feet up?" he asked.

"Take the signal flags for a pillow—the bag's hanging on the peg," I said.

That was better and he was quiet awhile. *Rudolfina* dipped and curtsied to the swell, her rigging sang and creaked and waves plashed cosily against her hull, right under my ear.

"Why does it keep going kluck kluck kluck all the time, like that?" asked Knut. "It never did in *Tanja III*."

"*Tanja* was carvel-built, but *Rudolfina* is clinker-built, you know, with one plank slightly overlapping the other," I tried to explain. "And when the waves lap up against the—"

"Yes, of course—ooooah!" yawned Knut, "blinker-built is much better. Who wants caramel-built, pooh! Ooooah!"

That was the last thing I heard for some time.

CHAPTER SEVEN

I WAS AWAKENED by a little naked foot trampling on my pillow and on my hair, giving it a hefty tug. I opened my eyes. It was Pysen.

"Go away," I said sleepily.

"Noho," he said. "You're lying on my flag. I'm going to hoist it because I'm awake now."

"Hush!" I said. "Talk very quietly and go and lie down. We're not going to get up for a long time. Besides, I'm not lying on any flag."

"Yes, you are, because there it is," he said, pointing.

It was quite true, the flag lay rolled up on the little shelf behind me. Rosalind's wrist watch was hanging from a hook. The time was a quarter to four.

"Listen, Pysen," I said. "If you'll go to sleep again for a bit you shall get up presently and go fishing with me for Persson."

"Yes, but I must hoist the flag first," said Pysen.

"You can't. The door's shut and you can't get out," I said.

"You can open it," said Pysen.

"No," I answered. "And you aren't wearing your life

jacket, and you know you mustn't go on deck without it."

"I'll fetch it and you can put it on," he said.

"Not now. It isn't morning yet; it's the middle of the night. Nobody hoists flags in the middle of the night. A proper flag officer wouldn't ever do that. Go and lie down and go to sleep."

He lay down beside me with his head on my pillow. He lay in a half-kneeling position, with his bottom sticking up, and squashed me up against the wall.

"I shall sleep here with you," he said firmly.

"There isn't room; I want to be left in peace," I said.

He made no reply, but continued to kneel with his face in the pillow, pretending to be asleep. I hadn't the heart to push him away, but oh, how I longed for my tent just then!

After about two and a half minutes, or so it seemed, he sat up again.

"Is it morning now?"

"No," I said. "Be quiet and go to sleep." He cuddled down obediently, this time lying face upward. A gleam of daylight fell across it from the skylight. He shut his eyes tightly, but after a while I noticed him watching me with them half open.

"Now it's time, isn't it?" he said triumphantly.

"Yes," I said, sighing, "it's morning now."

Perhaps the perch will be biting well at this time of

day, I thought. So we got up and dressed quietly so as not to disturb the others. I fixed Pysen's life jacket, took the flag, and climbed out through the doorway. Knut stirred and muttered but didn't wake. The sky was as pink as a strawberry ice, reflected in an equally pink mirror in a dark frame. The sun was up but still hidden behind the rock. The wind had died down, but out beyond the inlet little wavelets showed that a morning breeze was getting up. The deck was wet with dew as we made our way aft, Pysen ceremoniously carrying the flag. A little way aft of us lay *Dunkan*, and now I could see that she was gray and black, and that the deckhouse was green trimmed with white.

I got the rods and the can of bait, and when the flag was made fast we sat in the stern and baited our lines. That is to say, I put the bait on, of course, but then Pysen insisted I should leave his rod alone. But by the time he had drawn it in and tangled the line in the backstays several times, I had to help him.

"Will the fishes come soon?" he inquired.

"Not if you talk," I replied, and he was quiet for a bit.

"Look!" he said. "There's a teeny, teeny little man sitting there."

I looked up from my float. A punt was lying by the point and in it sat Kalle Hamper, fishing.

"That's quite a big 'uncle'," I said, for Kalle Hamper was about six feet tall. "He's called Kalle Hamper."

"Noho," said Pysen, "he's as tiny as that," and he showed me with his thumb and forefinger how small the old man was. He hadn't realized how distance affects things. Then his float bobbed down.

"Pysen!" I cried, "you've got a bite! Draw up, for goodness' sake!"

He tried hard but couldn't manage. "It's stuck!" he said, tugging at it. I had to come to the rescue. A perch, a really fine one. Pysen was delighted.

"My fish!" he said. "My very own little fish!" He patted it cautiously and pricked his finger on its back fin.

"It isn't nice," he said, frowning at it. "Nasty old fish!"

"Don't you want to go on fishing any longer, then?" I asked. But of course he did. He wanted to catch enough fish to fill Rudolfina. So we sat there till the sun came up over the rock and the bay turned gold and the fish tired of biting. By that time we had eight perch on the deck.

Kalle Hamper came rowing toward us.

"Morning!" said he. "Up already? And that little shrimp, too. Why, bless me if he isn't fishing as well!"

"Pysen, say how d'you do to Uncle Kalle."

"Just Kalle," said Kalle Hamper. He didn't like our calling him uncle.

Pysen stared at him, round-eyed. "The man was big!" he said to me.

Kalle had done well with his fishing. There was a fine feeding ground for perch just off the point, he said. Then he fetched the dinghy for us. He had to turn her upside down first, for she was full of water, though she had lain high up on the beach.

"Now I'm going to have a bit of a rest, and I think you'd better do likewise," said he.

The sun was already quite warm. I put the fish in the shade and drew up some water and we rinsed our hands and were just going to turn in when Rosalind came out. She had on her bathing suit, and she dived straight into the water. That made me want to do the same thing. The water was lovely and cool, and of course we had to dry ourselves in the sun afterward, and then Mirre woke up and came out yawning, and said, "Well, I never! I must have a dip too." Of course we went over the side again and then Knut came out, and when Knut is in the water I feel I must go in as well, so hey presto, in I went again and we dived and splashed and played pirates. But then we heard Dessi at the cabin door.

"I don't want to find fault, and it's certainly fun to swim, but surely you could do it at a reasonable hour so that other people could sleep," she said. "And as for you, Lars, I know you've been in three times already, and you know what they said at home about swimming too much, so I think it high time you came out. And the first one out can make the chocolate and bring me some in bed, with three or four pieces of bread and butter, then I'll forgive you for getting up and making a disturbance, for oh, am I hungry! Aren't the rest of you hungry, too?"

"Yes!" we shouted. But when we came out Dessi was

already standing by the primus preparing the chocolate.

"I was too hungry to wait for you," she said.

"Persson, come along, darling little Persson. You shall have some nice fish," said Pysen, catching sight of his dearly loved friend. But Persson only mewed and stared toward the shore. She has her regular habits and is accustomed to being let out first thing in the morning. Rosalind and Mirre rowed ashore with her.

The weather looked as if it were going to be fine. The pennant at the masthead showed the wind to be southwesterly.

"Remember," said Dessi, trying to sound severe, as we sat round the steaming mugs of chocolate, "remember that such late hours won't do. Tonight we shall all go to bed very early. And now we must find a telephone as soon as possible."

"Telephone!" said Knut. "Isn't this an uninhabited island, then?"

"Ha ha!" laughed Rosalind. "Haven't you looked at the chart? There's a village, or a lot of houses, anyway, the other side of the hill. There's sure to be a telephone."

"I'll go and call," said Knut. "I can buy milk at the same time and anything else we need."

"I'll come with you, anyway," said Dessi. "Mama will want to talk to me. But it's miles too early yet."

Knut didn't believe this. He said people were always up early in the country. And he persisted in wanting to go alone. I realized why.

"We can all go together," I said.

First we made the beds and tidied up a bit, and scrubbed the deck, and then we went ashore. We made two journeys, for the dinghy wouldn't hold all of us as well as the milk cans. Knut went up to the tent.

"You go on; I'll follow you," he said.

We found a little track leading down to the hamlet. There were only three small farms, but the people were up and about, and they had a telephone and said we might certainly use it. It took a little time getting through, so we sat and waited outside, and Dessi went down to the dairy and bought new milk. Then along came Knut. He had the briefcase with him. He scowled at me, rather, but I took no notice. He went down with Dessi, but soon came up again.

"Well?" I asked.

He made no reply but disappeared around the corner. Perhaps he thought that the girl who brought the milk was the wrong sort of native.

Then Dessi came with the milk, and just afterward we got through to them at home. They were very glad to hear us because they had scarcely been able to sleep for wondering how we were getting on in the storm. Dessi told them everything about Pysen and Persson and then we all had a word with Mama, except Knut, who had disappeared. We promised to call again soon, and the call was over.

We went back with our milk. On the way we picked wild strawberries. When we reached the shore we saw signs of activity aboard *Dunkan*. So we carried the baskets down from the tent and began loading them aboard. Kalle came with the punt and filled it so full of them that it looked like a dish full of meringues.

"They are all a bit stained with sea water," he said, examining them. "They look a trifle the worse for wear. I'll have to knock a bit off the price if I'm to get rid of them."

Vendla stood on board *Dunkan*, shaking the water from the potato saucepan and calling that breakfast was ready. We hadn't brought all the baskets, and Knut had still not put in an appearance, but it seemed a pity to let the food wait, so we piled aboard. The smell of fried perch was delicious, but that was nothing to the taste, for Vendla was a splendid cook.

She cut thick slices of bread for us.

"Put plenty of butter on," said Kalle.

"Don't worry, I will," said she, and put it on so thickly that there was more butter than bread.

"I don't worry," said Kalle. "Come on now, kids, eat up."

He didn't have to ask us twice.

"*Dunkan* ahoy!" sounded from the beach, and there stood Knut with his briefcase. It hadn't gotten any thinner, but looked just as full as ever, I noticed when I went to fetch him.

"How many looking glasses did you sell?" I asked.

"None," he replied. "But anyway, I sold a comb at the farm farthest off."

"You did? That was very good," I said.

"Mm," said Knut in reply, and that was all.

"What happened?"

"It wasn't much good. Do you know what she said, the one who bought it? She said it might do to comb her cat, which had gotten fleas. And then she haggled over the price. I only made ten öre on it. But don't tell the girls."

When we had finished our meal and washed up we went ashore and brought back the rest of the baskets. Dessi sat on the rock, sketching *Dunkan*, and Pysen lay asleep in Dessi's shadow.

"So you can paint pictures, eh?" said Kalle Hamper. "Are those real oil paints?"

"Yes," said Dessi. "I've just started using them, and it's great fun. I've only used water colors until now."

Kalle pondered awhile.

"I've always wanted to paint," he said. "Then I could paint flowers on all the little baskets and charge at least twenty-five öre more for them. It would be just the thing, at the moment. A few flowers would cover the stains."

"I'll have a shot at it," said Dessi. "I can always try."

Kalle was delighted. We had thought of moving on, actually, and so had he. But he said we were none of us bound to do so, so we stayed put all the morning. Dessi took her brushes and tubes and pencils across to *Dunkan*, and sat there painting baskets, and became very good friends with Vendla. Kalle fiddled about with the engine and hung the tarpaulins out to dry. Dessi's flowers didn't turn out quite as he had expected, but he said the chief

thing was that the baskets had been painted, and they were smart, very smart, and the summer visitors would most certainly buy them.

We didn't get off before about three o'clock. Kalle and Vendla were making for Nynäshamn, where Vendla was to stay for a time with a sister of hers who was ill, while Kalle went on alone, sailing among the islands. We agreed to keep a lookout for each other, for he intended going here, there and everywhere, and it seemed as if we were too.

Kalle chewed his pipe and started the blowlamp going. We said our good-byes and thanks and got into the dinghy and rowed over to *Rudolfina* and set sail, for there was a fair wind. We swept past *Dunkan* at a good speed and had gone a long way before Kalle got his stonka stonka started. But an engine is always an engine, and gradually *Dunkan* overtook us.

In the door of her little green cuddy stood Vendla, and waved her apron, and the smoke from the stack lay like a long tail in their wake, for Kalle drove his engine on kerosene. Kerosene smells better than crude oil actually.

"See you at Möja!" cried Kalle and waved his cap.

CHAPTER EIGHT

WHEN WE GOT CLEAR of the little islands around the inlet we ran before the wind. Rosalind steered and I studied the chart while Dessi and Mirre employed themselves by splicing rope ends in the fo'c'sle. Knut was making paper swallows for Pysen, who sent them overboard and cried, "More, more!" Then along came two steamers from the direction of Nyköping, and Rosalind steered as close to them as she dared, so that we got a real backwash.

Someone was standing waving on one of them. We thought it looked like a boy we knew. So Knut fetched Mama's old opera glasses from the cabin and jumped up on the gangway and began using them. We gazed after the boy, Rosalind and I, so we never noticed when the jibe came.

"Dreadful big . . ." screamed Pysen.

Just as Knut turned around, the boom hit him on the head and swept him overboard, glasses and all. It happened in a flash before we had time to realize it.

"Go about!" I shrieked. Rosalind put the helm hard over, the steamer reversed her engines and signaled: Toot! Toot! Toot! Dessi and Mirre came rushing up, both shouting at once, "He's gone down! I can't see him, he must have been knocked unconscious! Oh, Knut!"

I lay half across the gunwale, boat hook in hand, and Mirre seized the lifebuoy and held it in readiness. Rosalind, white-lipped, stood trying to maneuver the boat to where Knut had disappeared.

High above everything sounded Pysen's despairing cry, "Dreadful big boom boom! I *did* call dreadful big boom boom to him!"

He was knocked unconscious, I thought, and must have swallowed a lot of water and gone to the bottom like a stone. No, that couldn't happen to any of us! It isn't true. Not Knut!

They were preparing to launch a lifeboat from the steamer, now. We stared . . . stared. And then—there! A good bit farther west than I had guessed, we caught sight of him all at once. We shouted, we laughed, we cheered. Mirre pulled the dinghy alongside and I jumped down into it so quickly that it shipped water and started turning around.

"Hurry! Hurry!" screamed Dessi, and Rosalind flung the lifebuoy after me so that it hit me on the head. But Mirre cried, "He's swimming! D'you see? He's swimming!"

The lifeboat and I reached him at the same moment. The two men from the steamer tried to haul him up, but he dodged a little and caught hold of the dinghy's stern instead. He was so exhausted that he couldn't get in without help, but I got him aboard at last. He was bleeding from the nose and mouth and blowing like a pair of bellows, and he fell in a little heap on the bottom of the dinghy, coughing and spitting out sea water and blood.

They waved to us from the lifeboat, and rowed back to the steamer. Knut didn't seem to notice anything.

"You were lucky," I said. I couldn't find anything better to say. He only grunted and went on spitting. But when we got back to *Rudolfina* and climbed on board, he said, "I've lost Mama's glasses."

"Forget the glasses!" exclaimed Mirre. "We could die of relief that you are all right."

It was true. And the girls said that he must go and lie down, for he must be rather concussed after getting such a blow. But he went down into the cabin, looked at himself in the glass, came out again, and said, "My face is a bit swollen, isn't it?" That was a mild way of putting it. His lip was split and his nose looked like a pink potato.

We fell off and ran before the wind, coming to a narrow channel where buoys stood close as fence posts. It took a lot of dodging and maneuvering, and I was so taken up with it that I had no time to dwell much on what had happened to Knut, beyond thinking, "Supposing the worst had happened, what should we have done and felt?"

He had gone down to have a rest at last. The channel opened out again in the distance, but then we came to Västra Stendörren, where it formed a big S among the buoys and rocks. It was fun but rather confusing, and we had no time to eat anything, however famished we felt.

Pysen complained lustily and was pacified temporarily by being given a box of cookies. The rest of us were silent, saying nothing except, "Going about . . . Slack away the sheet, Rosalind . . . Let her fall off again . . . Jibe coming . . . carry on, Mirre."

But when we reached a bay, Dessi set about filleting Pysen's and my perch and preparing lunch. She's good at that, though in other ways Mirre is the better cook. We couldn't yet light the primus, for the wind was fresh and we wanted to take advantage of it, so *Rudolfina* lay over with her port gunwale almost awash.

"*Usch!*" said Pysen, bracing his feet, "the boat mustn't go crooked—noho!"

Persson climbed cautiously around to the starboard side, pressing herself from time to time against the cabin, and shaking herself when the spray wet her every now and then.

We coasted along the southeast side of the bay before dropping anchor in a cove by Sävsundet. Before we had lowered the sails the perch were frying in the pan, for Mirre can work wonders when she is really hungry. We were pretty tired but stimulated by the thought of food. And when Knut was about to bite into a cheese sandwich, he said, "It's gone!"

"What's gone?" we asked.

"The tooth, my loose tooth!" He felt for it, first with his tongue, then his finger.

"Yes, it's gone all right," he said. "It must have gone when the boom hit me."

"Now you won't have to go to the dentist," said Mirre. "The boom did the job instead."

"A pretty rough dentist," said Dessi. "He used rather more force than he needed to do, I should say."

"Knut," said Rosalind, "aren't you glad?"

"Of course," said Knut, his split lip widening in a grin. "It's nice being rid of it. I shall be able to eat on both sides soon. Though just at present it doesn't feel too good."

"I didn't mean about the tooth," said Rosalind. "I meant aren't you thankful that everything turned out all right?"

"Of course," he mumbled, looking down at his feet.

"What did it feel like when you fell?" I asked.

"I don't know, I didn't have time to think. It happened so quickly and hurt so much, and then I just went down and got a gulp of cold water and went under and came up again. And at first I couldn't swim at all and of course I was a bit scared, but not for long. Though it was horrid. But if you can swim, well . . . And you can bet your boots I'll watch out for the boom, now."

"I think we all shall," said Dessi.

"A pity about Mama's glasses," said Knut. "Listen, does anyone want this last fillet? If not, I'll have it."

"Yes, you have it," we all said with one voice.

"Now I think we'll celebrate," said Mirre, a little later. "It's the right sort of occasion. Aunt Bella gave us a chocolate cake to have on Pysen's birthday tomorrow. But I think we'll have half of it today, don't you? Perhaps we can find something else to feast Pysen with. And the cake will be fresher today. What do you say, Pysen? Shall we have the cake?"

Pysen nodded. "My cake," said he. "You can all have some. Lots and lots."

"Good," said Dessi. "And we'll have fruit drinks, too."

The cake was great, like everything Aunt Bella makes. There wasn't much wrong with the fruit drinks, either. But we all felt rather strained and serious as we sat there. We realized that Mirre had hit on this celebration so that we should forget all about that ghastly moment when we couldn't see Knut and didn't know whether we ever would again.

We didn't go ashore and put up the tent that night. I lay on the sail bag and Knut had the hammock in the fo'c'sle. The girls didn't want us to be away from them. We went to bed early, but I didn't sleep at all well. There were masses of mosquitoes in Sävsundet and they searched us out and whined and bothered us and sucked our young blood, so that in the morning we all looked as if we had measles.

But it wasn't only the mosquitoes that had made it difficult to get to sleep. It was the thought, "How easily it can happen!"

CHAPTER NINE

PYSEN WAS WAKENED with songs and flowers next morning. We had all the flags put out in honor of the yeoman of signals. He was delighted.

"Is *Rudolfina* a Christmas tree now?"

"A birthday tree," said Rosalind.

"But I want to put them up myself, yoho, because *I'm* the flagsiffer." But we promised he should haul them all down himself that evening instead.

"Will it be evening soon?" he asked.

The girls had gotten up quietly very early and rowed ashore and picked vetch and cranesbill and buttercups, and woven a long garland of them and twined it around our outside dining table, "the kennel." There was a plate heaped with wild strawberries as well. They had "written" "Pysen, 4 years," in little green leaves near the birthday child's mug. Then we brought out our presents. A drawing book with colored chalks from Dessi; a little garage made from a cigar box, for Fimbo and Lyxen, from me; a bib with three rabbits, which Rosalind and Mirre had sewed; and a brightly colored beach ball, a big one, from Papa and Mama. Knut gave him one of the little ducks out of the briefcase.

"Look," said Pysen. "My duck has had a puppy."

"It's a widgeon," said Knut.

"Widdy John," said Pysen, and always called it that, afterward.

We stayed in Sävsundet until next morning. We thought Pysen would enjoy having a little time ashore on his birthday. We swam twice, and practiced swimming

movements with him. He got on well. He wasn't a bit afraid.

"He'll be swimming like a frog before his next birthday," said Rosalind. And we all felt sure he would.

Then he played with the beach ball and the duck and duckling, and I went to look for a telephone. Knut had no desire to come this time. His face looked as if he had been in a fight. Dessi had treated his cut lip with iodine and put plaster on it. His nose had turned blue and black and green, and was pretty tender.

We had decided not to alarm our parents by telling them how Knut had fallen overboard. Not only could the affair not be undone, but they might be so frightened that they would order us back home at once.

"We won't say anything about it until we get back home again," we said. "We'll write it up in the logbook and they will be able to read about it there."

But when I got Mama on the line she began asking how we all were. When she got to Knut, she asked, "Has he lost his tooth yet?" and I said "yes." I couldn't lie to her.

"What happened? Did he pull it out himself?" she asked.

"N-no," I said.

"Oh. Well, which of you pulled it out, then?" she asked.

"None of us," I said, beginning to sweat, for I thought she would get the whole story out of me, and then good-bye to the entire trip. I would have to joke about it, I thought, and then perhaps she wouldn't be scared.

"Well, it was . . . it was a dentist," I said.

"A dentist? Where did Knut come across a dentist?"

"Aboard *Rudolfina*. He's still there."

"Well, I never," said Mama, and I heard her say to somebody, probably Aunt Bella, "They seem to have run across a dentist on their trip."

"Did he charge anything for pulling out the tooth, Lars?"

"No, it didn't cost anything," I replied.

"How very kind of him! What is his name?"

I had to think quickly. Should I say Boom? But then she might guess. No, wait a second—But isn't a boom made of wood?

"His name is Wood," I said. "He comes from the west coast."

"The dentist is a Dr. Wood from the west coast," said Mama to Aunt Bella. "Give him my kind regards and thank him very much, Lars. And give them all my love, and take care of yourselves. And call again soon."

Knut and the girls were very tickled when I told them about Dr. Wood the dentist. Today we were able to laugh about it all. The dentist touch had lightened up the whole story.

We sunbathed and had a marvelous day and didn't forget to cook three proper meals. We built sand castles for Pysen and made boats of bark and rushes, and indulged him in every way known to model brothers and sisters. We carried him pickaback, and played at being grebes, and swam about with him on our backs. It was hard work, for Pysen does not easily tire, and we told each other it was lucky he didn't have a birthday every day. At last he went to sleep under an alder, and didn't wake up when Dessi made a drawing of him, nor when we carried him to the dinghy and rowed him back to *Rudolfina* and laid him down. So it had been a satisfactory birthday. Then I spent the evening recording everything that had happened in the logbook.

The following morning at six o'clock we weighed anchor and sailed away from Sävsundet. The fine weather held, and so did the southwest wind. Soon the channel widened and we began to see open water here and there. Suddenly the whole Baltic opened to the south, in a billowing plain of rippling greeny-blue. We had a following wind and made good speed out toward Landsort. For a moment we wondered whether to sail out to the lighthouse, but the sea was very rough there and Pysen protested vigorously against "Sailing all on one side" again.

"I've never seen a flag officer frightened of a bit of a sea!" said Rosalind. Dessi asked her how many she had seen.

"Sh!" replied Rosalind, "I'm only educating him a bit."

"I'm not afraid, noho," said Pysen, "but I don't want to fall in the water. Only when I go swimming."

"It's a good thing you are careful," I said. "But sometimes we have to sail on one side, you know, and it isn't dangerous."

But Dessi said it would be better to keep inside the skerries in any case, as long as the sea looked like that.

"We can go through the Herrhamra passage," she said, pointing on the chart.

I shaped course in a more easterly direction. But the waves got higher and higher and Pysen started to bellow. I don't wonder he was scared, for it was a really ugly sea. We still had some way to go before reaching the Herrhamra passage. The boat bucked, the waves splashed over us, and Mirre had a tough job with the pumping.

"We can't make it, we'll have to go more northerly," I yelled to Dessi and put the helm up. There were heaps of islets and rocks ahead of us. On the other side of the rocks we glimpsed a channel marked by three buoys. But between us and it the waves broke high over the shallows to right and left.

"Boo-hoo!" wailed Pysen.

"Dare we? It looks so awful," said Dessi. "Hush, Pysen darling!"

"We must," I said. "We have to keep between the second and third buoy—it's shown clearly on the chart."

Dessi hastily reached for the life belts and drew Pysen to her. Mirre rushed down into the cabin, and when she returned she was wearing her bathing cap.

"I've got the money here," she cried, pointing to a big square bulge beneath it. It was the wallet.

Rudolfina flew toward the opening like a rocket. Every

second I expected a crash and something even worse. For were she to go aground at that speed there would be little left of her but matchwood. I turned her hard aport and she jibed.

"Boo-hoo!" howled Pysen. "Dreadful big boo-hoo!"

And then we were through the opening and in the lee of the islands. No more waves, no more treacherous hidden rocks. Only a light wind, and then plain sailing through the channel and past the buoys. Pysen's mouth closed at last. "It's all right now," he said, sniffing a bit.

"My gracious! It's exciting, sailing," said Mirre when she had removed her bathing cap and put the life belts back in the seat under the well.

"Next time we'll reef the sails before making for the open sea in such a strong wind," said Dessi. "It would have been a fine thing if the sail had torn."

"I never thought we'd have to shorten sail for a little bit of a blow like that," I said.

"Neither did I," said Mirre, "and when I realized it, it was too late to do anything about it."

But Dessi said, "D'you know what? We've all been too slack—especially me. We never were so careless aboard *Tanja III*."

"No, because the dye manager was always there to tell us what to do," I said.

"We've obviously got to look out for ourselves now," said Rosalind.

"And remind each other," said Dessi. "My dears, tell me whenever you think I'm sitting with my head in the clouds."

"I'll give you a nudge," said Pysen.

"Bless you, ducky," said Dessi, trying to kiss him. He wriggled away.

"Flagsiffers don't never get kissed, noho," said he.

"Are you sure of that?" asked Dessi, laughing.

"Noho. I mean yes indeed. Because people don't ever kiss them. When are we having something to eat? I'm dreadful hungry. You said we were going to have pancakes today."

"So I did," said Dessi. "I was going to beat up the batter so that the flour would have time to swell—Are you down there, Knut? Be a dear and get out a packet of dried milk."

"Don't bother, I got it ready ages ago," said Mirre. "You can start frying whenever you like."

Mirre was our prize cook. She liked it so much that she would quietly set about preparing food even when it was somebody else's turn. Dessi is often glad to get out of it. Actually she only enjoys messing about with green salads and tomatoes and radishes and things that are pretty to look at. And Mama says nobody can make a table look as charming as Dessi can. But when you want a really satisfying meal, Mirre's the one for the job. Rosalind isn't bad at it, either, though she generally plumps for fried sausages, as that's the easiest.

"Tomorrow morning early, we'll go into Nynäshamn," said Mirre as she greased the frying pan with buttered paper. "Then we'll buy milk and new buns."

"And I'll treat you to ices," I said.

"Thanks—a chocolate one for me, please," said Rosalind.

"And me," said Knut.

The others wanted the ordinary kind. Pysen wanted two for himself and "one for Persson, yes indeed, because she likes them too."

"We can't have more than one each," I said. "If you have two somebody will have to go without."

"Not Persson. Persson likes ices," said Pysen.

"We all do," said I, "but Persson will have to have one to herself, of course."

There were fewer islands now, and Viksten's lighthouse hove into sight. The sea grew rather rough again. The lighthouse soon vanished from sight as we scurried along to Järflotta as quick as we could.

That night we lay in a bay near Trehörningen. Next morning we donned our shoregoing clothes—that is to say, "we men" as Pysen puts it, wore clean shorts, and the girls fished out their crumpled dresses, thinking they looked smarter in them than in shorts. And we rowed in to Nynäshamn. Persson came too, and for safety's sake Mirre had made a little leash for her so that she shouldn't run away. She went as sedately as a dog on the leash and had her ice, eating it all up and licking her lips for more, like the rest of us.

Outside the baker's where we bought the buns we ran across Vendla. She seemed awfully pleased.

"Well, I never, how nice to see you again," she said. "Do you know, Kalle sold nearly all the painted baskets here in Nynäshamn. People were crazy about them. Now he doesn't know how he's going to get any more like them. He said he would pay you well if he could get in touch with you again."

"Where is he now, then?" asked Dessi.

"He left for Mysingen early yesterday. He means to go inland here, there, and everywhere; he talked of Utö and Ornö and Nämdö and all the rest of it, and of course he's going to Möja, he always does."

"We're going there, too," said Mirre. "Aren't we, everyone?"

"Of course," we said, "we're going to Möja, of course."

"Well, keep a lookout for him, then," said Vendla, "for as I say, he does so want to meet you again and get some more paintings."

Then she invited us all to have ices. And of course we accepted and were careful not to let on that we had already had some. Dessi nudged Rosalind and Knut and said, "Woe betide you if you breathe a word about chocolate ones!" When we went to the kiosk and the girl there asked what kind we wanted, we chose ordinary ones because they were the cheapest. But then Pysen spoiled the show, because he said, "Persson wants another ice as well."

"Hush, Pysen," we said.

"A cat can't eat ices, my dear child!" said Vendla, laughing.

"Oh yes, indeed she can eat ices. She just ate a whole one, so there," said Pysen.

"Pysen dear, let me help you take the paper off yours," said Mirre hurriedly. But the girl in the kiosk, who naturally wanted to sell her ices, said, "Oh yes, madam, all cats like vanilla ice. It's quite true, this one's just eaten a whole one and finished it off before you could say knife."

Then Vendla laughed until the wrinkles showed in her cheeks, and said, "Well, Persson must have another, of course." We thought how nice she was. She knew we had had ices already but she invited us to have some more.

"Ices are so delicious," we said apologetically, "especially on such a hot day."

"That may be," she replied, "but for my part I find they just give me a toothache."

We finished our ices—so did Persson—and said thank you and good-bye to Vendla. She had to get back to her sick sister, she said.

Mirre rowed out to *Rudolfina* with Rosalind and Knut and Pysen. Dessi and I sat on the beach and waited to be fetched.

"Say, Lars," said Dessi, "why not let's go and look for Kalle Hamper as soon as possible?"

"Well, we can, of course," I said. "Do you think it's such fun painting baskets?"

"Oh, that . . ." she replied. "No, but how would it be if we sailed with him? I mean, he is just cruising around

and landing here and there, and that's exactly what we thought of doing."

"Wasn't it you who was so eager to be alone?" I asked.

"Yes, but he is so nice. He wouldn't be tiresome or get in the way at all."

"Well, we might," I said. "But you know he's selling baskets and that means he'll only go around the islands where there are plenty of people; otherwise he'd do no business. And we meant to visit the uninhabited ones."

"Well, we can do that too, of course," said Dessi. "But so much can happen in a whole month. And after that business with Knut I think it would be nice to have a grown-up person at hand sometimes.

Then we talked about other things for a bit.

We had a marvelous sail up toward Mysingen, and counted one big island after another among the ones screening the bay from the Baltic. We sailed past Nåtarö and saw Danziger Gatt and the open sea, and then came Rånö, which means "Robbery Island" and we thought it sounded so sinister that nobody except Knut wanted to land there. So we voted against him and went on to Utö and entered the narrow harbor and came to rest in the cover behind Persholmen. Neither there nor anywhere on the way there did we catch sight of *Dunkan*.

We landed on the island and went to look at the old mine shaft, now full of water, looking very black and strange. I asked Rosalind, who is our champion swimmer number one, if she would like to swim there, but she said no thanks! She thought it seemed uncanny and as though some fearsome monster might come and drag one down into that eerie lake.

It was getting late already, so Dessi went back aboard with Pysen and the rest of us traipsed over the island and swam in the real sea. It was a still, warm evening and it was hard to leave the lukewarm water. But when we had done so we made haste to get into our clothes, for we were attacked by a swarm of bloodthirsty mosquitoes which feasted on us more persistently than any we had yet come across. Matters didn't improve much even at night, for both aboard *Rudolfina* and in our tent the bloodsuckers searched us out. In the morning, the walls of the fo'c'sle were decorated with the corpses of mosquitoes which Rosalind had slain with a rolled-up newspaper. Later in the day we found the bottle of jungle oil Mama had given us, for which we had searched all through *Rudolfina*. Pysen had discovered it and hidden it in his box of blocks because the label on it was so pretty.

All that day we swam, refusing to think of parental injunctions. We simply had to swim, because it was the only thing that stopped the itching. And though we had found the jungle oil and didn't need to worry about being bitten anymore, we had no desire to listen to the noise of mosquitoes again that night, so after lunch we set out for Mysingen bay once more.

We hadn't been going long before the wind dropped. Not a breath, not the faintest hint of a breath. But instead of starting up the engine we hit on something much better. We got the life belts and jumped in, all except Dessi and Pysen, and then we lay on our backs, floating around *Rudolfina* for hours. Like waterlilies, said Rosalind. Like dumplings in the soup, said Mirre. We laughed and screamed and shouted to each other. The sails hung limp and the boat lay as motionless as a painting, and the sun shone and the gulls sat having an afternoon nap on the rocks. In the cabin Pysen lay asleep, and on deck sat Dessi, palette in hand, painting a tangle of seaweed which we had thrown up to her. Up and down and around and around the deck paced Persson, gazing anxiously at us, wondering what we were doing in the water which she so much disliked. "Miaow!" she said time and time again. "Miaow!"

Then all at once the wind freshened, the sail bellied, and the water began creaming round the bow. *Rudolfina* sailed away from the waterlilies and dumplings before we realized what was happening. It didn't worry us at all.

Dessi, poor girl, sat there painting seaweed, not noticing at first how erratically *Rudolfina* was behaving. Then came a jibe and Dessi sprang up and gazed horror-struck, first at the sail and then at us, then leapt for the tiller and sheet. She steered back to us as deftly as if she had never been doing anything else all her life. Sometimes Dessi is absent-minded, but few people can think more quickly than she can, if necessary.

Persson fled below deck when we, the sea gods, came splashing over the gunwale. She thought nothing could be more horrid than such wet creatures trying to stroke a dainty little cat's dry fur. She hated water. But she loved sunning herself on the cabin roof. She would sit there for hours, perfectly still, with her tail curled around her paws, like a little statue, reveling in the sun. When we had been ashore she was generally the first to jump into the dinghy again. *Rudolfina* had obviously become her real home.

But that evening when we went ashore on Ornö, Persson disappeared. We called and coaxed and reproached one another because nobody had thought of putting her on the leash. Pysen called and coaxed and the rest of us searched everywhere, but not a sign of Persson did we see. It grew dark and we thought of putting our tent up, and asked an old man for permission to do so, but he said he didn't want anyone camping there, so Knut and I went back to the boat and slept in the fo'c'sle.

"Tomorrow we'll go over the island with a fine-toothed comb till we find Persson," said Dessi.

"Ornö's a big island," I said.

"Maybe, but we can't leave without the cat," said Mirre. "What would Aunt Bella say?"

"We'll stay here the whole month, if necessary, and not bother about sailing any farther," said Dessi, "but of course the cat will come back. We know our Persson."

Pysen howled himself to sleep. Neither the duck nor Widdy John could console him. Knut lent him both the little ducks he had in his briefcase, but he merely bemoaned his Persson.

"Now she'll have to stay out all night," he sobbed.

"Cats like doing that sometimes," said Rosalind. "They are creatures of the night; they can see in the dark."

"She was so clever," wept Pysen. "She could eat ices!"

"Well, so can you, but that doesn't mean you are clever," said Knut.

"Pysen is very clever," said Mirre, "and he shall have two ices with me as soon as we reach somewhere where they sell them."

"Persson, too," said Pysen instantly.

"Of course," we all promised.

At long last he fell asleep, and gradually so did the rest of us.

CHAPTER TEN

DURING THE NIGHT I heard a slight rattling at the anchor chain. Surely the wind wasn't getting up? I stuck my head out of the fo'c'sle door. But *Rudolfina* lay still and the water wasn't even rippling. The night was fine. Mysingen lay like an inky-blue tray of glass, and the wind was asleep.

But hush! There was a faint rattle from the chain again. Mysterious! Could someone be trying to climb up the side? When we swam we were in the habit of climbing aboard with the help of the chain. I crept out, almost expecting to see a pair of coarse hands on the chain, and a bearded face with a dagger between its teeth, hoisting itself over the gunwale, for I had been reading one of Knut's pirate books the previous evening. But I saw no pirate. I leaned over the railing and stared down at the chain which disappeared into the depths. Nothing was to be seen except a little trembling ripple ruffling the surface. Something had just been there—a sea bird, perhaps, or possibly a seal. Imagine if it had been a seal that had dived and would soon come up again! The ripple continued alongside *Rudolfina*, going toward her stern. I tiptoed along the side and reconnoitered.

Hush, now I heard something! A faint, very faint splashing. That something, whatever it was, was amusing itself by swimming around Rudolfina. Now it had reached the dinghy. Surely whoever it was didn't think of stealing it!

I jumped up—and caught sight of the swimmer.

"Persson!" I cried.

It was Aunt Bella's precious cat, plowing the water with paddling forepaws, anxiously trying to climb up the dinghy's painter as she had failed to manage the anchor chain. Now she was swimming rapidly toward me. Her eyes looked large and frightened, her whiskers were quivering.

Dessi's bathing cape was hanging over the boom to dry. I took it and threw it down to act as a rope ladder. The cat dug her claws in and clung to it as I drew it up. Water poured off her as she reached the deck. I was preparing to pick her up and dry her, but she didn't give me a chance. She ran off and rushed around and around the deck like a mad thing. Then she saw the open door of the fo'c'sle and rushed in there. I followed.

There was a terrified shriek at first when the wet cat jumped up onto her friend Pysen.

"What's that?" asked sleepy voices from all sides.

"It's Persson!" cried Pysen jubilantly. "Clever little Persson! She's wetting in my bed—for shame, Persson!"

"Persson swam aboard," said I.

"Don't try and be funny," said Knut, "Persson, who's

so terrified of water! It was you who went ashore and fetched her."

I explained what had happened.

"Darling, clever little Persson, who can swim!" said Pysen.

"Just think," said Rosalind, "she hates the water, but she loves us and *Rudolfina* so much that it overcame her natural cat instincts. I think it's fine."

"Persson is a cat full of character," said Dessi.

"*Atishoo!*" sneezed Pysen, whose tummy was chilled by the wet cat. Mirre got up and put dry clothes in his bunk and dried poor Persson and gave her some milk.

Early next morning we set sail. We thought we'd take Persson ashore first, but she wasn't having any. She went and hid behind the ropes in the fo'c'sle and stayed crouching there all day. She had evidently been extremely frightened, because she wouldn't come out even for food.

"Better leave her alone to get over it," said Dessi.

But she didn't get over it. She stayed there all day.

"Animals that are unhappy or sick always creep away into a dark corner," said Rosalind. "I think she caught a chill from her wetting."

We tried to drag her out, but she crept farther behind the cable locker. It was almost impossible to reach her. There were two bags of cotton waste there, stowed away at the back, and Persson's golden eyes shone over the top of them like the headlights of a toy locomotive. Rosalind wriggled in and tempted her with some canned cream, and she drank it but remained where she was and took no notice of our coaxing. We bought freshly caught herring from a fisherman at Utö, cleaned them and tried to entice her out to eat the heads and the insides, which she liked better than anything. But she remained in her dark retreat. Not even the smell of frying herrings when Mirre prepared the supper could entice out this Spartan.

At home she was almost glued to the stove when Aunt Bella did any cooking.

"There's something very odd about this," said Dessi when we turned in.

"She'll starve to death," said Rosalind.

"When she gets really famished she'll come out," I said.

The journey up to Nämdö and Runmarö went like a steamer trip. The wind was slight, and we lay around on deck, lazing, sunning ourselves, eating, and drinking fruit squashes. We were all burnt as brown as Aunt Bella's gingerbread. Knut's lip was quite healed and he had started fussing with his briefcase again.

The Runmarö coast looked steep and uninviting, so we went on till we came to an island where we found a lovely bay for swimming, facing Kanholmsfjärden and all the white sails out there. We dived in from the boat and lay out on the rocks to dry. When Mirre was getting into the dinghy with Pysen, Persson came out at last. We put on her leash and took her ashore for a scratch around. She looked miserable and unkempt.

"She's gotten awfully thin," said Rosalind. "Look how she's fallen away."

"Miaow!" said Persson, pulling at her leash and trying to get back into the dinghy as soon as she had finished.

"You're hungry, poor little thing," said Rosalind, "I can tell. Come, Persson, we'll get you something to eat."

I told Knut to go and look for a spring and ask if we

might have some water, for ours was finished. And I went on board to fetch the basket with the demijohn.

Persson ate two perch and two fried herrings and a whole mug of "funny milk," as Pysen called the dried milk which we whipped up when we couldn't get any fresh. Then she slunk off to her lair behind the chain locker again.

Knut was gone a long time. Then he came tearing along as though he had a wild animal after him. He rushed into the water and did a crawl stroke out to *Rudolfina*. He was absolutely winded when he got aboard.

"Well?" I asked. "How about the water?"

"Water? Oh, of course, the water. I forgot about it. But of course we can have some."

When I came up on deck with the demijohn and went to get the dinghy, he had already taken it and was on his way ashore again.

"Hi! Wait!" I called. He waved.

"I'll be back in a moment," he cried, rowing so that the oars leapt from the oarlocks.

"That boy!" I said to Rosalind. "He might just as well have fetched the water for once, since he was going ashore. He evidently thought this bottle would be too heavy, but he could have waited for me."

"I can't imagine what on earth he wants that old briefcase for on land," said Rosalind.

Knut was running over the rocks. He had the briefcase with him.

"Aha!" I said. "He's hoping to do business again."

I shouted, and Mirre took the dinghy and fetched us and the demijohn, and we went up to a cottage and asked for and were given some water. When we struggled down to the dinghy again we saw Knut coming back. He was in no hurry now but he was going as slowly and carefully as an old tortoise. In one hand he carried the briefcase. In the other he was carrying something that seemed especially wonderful, for he stopped and gazed at it with every step he took.

"What have you got there?" we inquired and crowded around him, Dessi, Mirre, and Pysen as well. But we didn't need to ask. It was something so marvelous that we couldn't say anything except, "Oh, Knut!"

It was a full-rigged ship in a bottle. We had always longed for one but without any hope of ever owning one. They are very rare and becoming rarer. The dye manager had one, but this one was exceptionally beautiful.

"Where did you get that?" I asked.

"Bartered it with one of the natives," said he. "You said I shouldn't be able to do any bartering, but what do you say now?"

"Terrific," I replied.

"And what did you give for it?" asked Dessi uneasily.

"Ah, what do you think?" swaggered Knut.

"Not glass beads, surely," I said.

"I did, though," he replied, pluming himself even more.

"You can't be serious," I said faintly.

"He's a businessman all right," said Rosalind.

"Glass beads! Impossible!" said Dessi.

"I gave her four bags," said Knut with a sigh. "But the boat's worth it."

"Wonderful!" said Mirre.

"Who was the native?" asked Dessi.

"A girl," he answered. "I shall put this on my bookcase at home and get Papa to make a stand for it."

"I want a nice bottle boat too," said Pysen.

"Didn't I tell you the natives liked glass beads?" said Knut to me, gloating over his bottle.

"Yes," I replied, "but that girl must be absolutely crazy! To exchange a rare, valuable thing like that for a few glass beads!"

"Well, there were four bags of them," said Knut.

Then we went on board and had another meal. The bottle with the schooner stood on the table, and we sat gazing devoutly at it, hardly believing it was really there. We sat trying to make out which was the flying jib and which the mizzen. And Mirre tried to figure out how the maker had got everything into place inside the bottle.

It was my turn to wash up, so I set to work. As I was standing rinsing things in the bucket I saw a rowing boat shoot out from behind the headland near where we swam and come straight toward us. A man in naval officer's uniform was rowing, and in the stern sat a little girl, crying. She looked about six or seven years old.

"Hullo, there!" said the officer to me. "Was it you who ran off with our beautiful bottle boat?"

Well, that sounded nice, I must say! I began to realize that all was not as it should be.

"N-no," I said, hesitantly, "it wasn't me."

"No, it wasn't him," sobbed the little girl, "and you did say the stupid old bottle belonged to me, Daddy."

"Oh!" cried Dessi from behind me. "What have you been up to, Knut?"

Knut climbed up onto the seat. He was red-faced and crestfallen.

"She said it was hers," he said bitterly. "She did say so."

The officer scratched his ear in a puzzled fashion.

"Yes, that's true; it is hers. But one can't go and cheat little girls out of their belongings like that. You know that very well."

"I didn't cheat her; she wanted to swap it," said Knut.

"Knut will give the bottle back at once, of course," said Dessi, her face as red as Knut's.

But the child in the boat wept in torrents. "I don't want the old bottle," she said, "it's a boy's toy. You always give me boys' things, Daddy. I'd much rather have the beads. I've never had any beads."

Knut, looking very cast down, fetched the bottle and handed it to the officer.

"I shall keep my beads, anyway," screamed the little girl.

"Quiet, Ingalill," said the officer. "And now I should like to get to the bottom of all this about the beads."

Knut said nothing, but Ingalill made up for it.

"I shall thread them and make a necklace, I tell you," she howled. "I love them; they are sweet. And beads are for girls."

As Knut remained silent, I explained matters. I said he was a businessman and that he had wanted to barter goods with the natives during our trip, and that he had read somewhere that they liked glass beads better than anything.

"Oh, shut up, will you," muttered Knut between his teeth.

Then I saw the officer biting his lip and trying not to laugh. He managed to look grave.

Rosalind came to the rescue.

"And you must realize, please, Admiral, that we have always longed for a ship in a bottle, like this one, and Knut couldn't resist it."

"No, I understand that," he said. "And by the way, I am only a captain at present. I bought that ship from one of the pilots at Sandhamn last week because I couldn't resist it either. I had rather a job, because the chap didn't want to sell it."

"So there's no chance of our being able to buy it, then?" asked Dessi. "I mean for cash. We haven't very much, but we could chip in together and give you all except the housekeeping money."

"Impossible," he replied. "It's true that my dear daughter says she doesn't care for it at present. But I'm pretty sure she'll change her mind before she's much older. So I think we'll keep it for her. And now, please give back the beads, Ingalill!"

The little girl cried and protested but gave back the beads to her father at last. "I've begun to thread them already," she sobbed. "I've only got three bags left."

"If you'll stop blubbering you can keep the one you've opened," said Knut with very bad grace. He looked very gloomy. Then he took the other three bags and went into the cabin.

The captain offered me a krona. "Give him that for the beads," he said.

"No, thank you," said Dessi quickly. "Knut mustn't be paid for being so silly. He meant no harm, but it was very foolish of him."

"Besides, those beads only cost thirty-five öre a bag," said Rosalind.

"Then we owe you many thanks," said the captain.

"Thank you for the beads," called the little girl to Knut. He didn't answer. Through the cabin door I could see that he had flung himself down on the bunk.

"That's a nice koster of yours," said the officer. "Have you got an engine as well?"

I said she had an old Bruzaholmer.

"Bruzaholmer, eh," he said. "What a remarkable coincidence! You don't come across them so often nowadays, but this morning I happened to be aboard a barge that had one."

"It wasn't Kalle Hamper's old *Dunkan*, by any chance?" said Dessi. "Were there baskets aboard?"

"Baskets? Yes, as a matter of fact there were. I bought a basket chair for the verandah, that's why I went aboard."

"Where was she?" asked Dessi.

"Up in the Möja channel."

"How far is that from here?" asked Dessi and began reckoning it up on the chart.

"I have a racing yacht that does seventeen knots, so I've been all round Möja in little more than an hour," he said. "But it would take quite an hour and a half for your Bruzaholmer to reach Möja Sound."

"We *sail*," said Rosalind, her nose a trifle in the air. "We only use the engine when there isn't a scrap of wind."

"I understand," said the officer, smiling slightly.

"Did Kalle Hamper say where he was making for?" I asked.

"I didn't ask him. But he's a nice old boy. Is he a friend of yours?"

"Yes," we said, and told him about the night it had blown baskets.

"What fun you're having on your trip," he said when we had finished. We said we certainly were. And some of us went on to tell him about Dr. Wood, the dentist, and someone else about Persson swimming back to the boat, and he said, "You are lucky," and it sounded as though he were a bit envious.

He asked where we were going next, and we said we hadn't any definite plans beyond just sailing here and there, and that we wanted to see Möja because such fine strawberries were grown there.

"Most of the Möja strawberries are cultivated in the little islands round about," he said. Then something seemed to strike him. "Say," he began, then broke off. "No, never mind. That boy in there, is his name Knut?"

"Yes," we said.

"Hey, Knut," he called. "Have you anything to sell?" Knut merely mumbled something. I said that he had, but that it was no good trying to talk to him just at present. Then the captain said good-bye and rowed away. The little girl had stopped crying. When they reached the shore she climbed up on a rock and waved to us.

"Hard luck on Knut," said Rosalind. "I think that child was stupid. She must have known one couldn't go and swap a lovely thing like that."

"Knut ought to have known that, too," said Dessi. "If I had had any idea he had gotten the bottle from such a small child, of course I would have sent him back with it immediately."

"I *said* it was a girl!" shouted Knut.

"Yes, but you didn't say how old she was."

"Don't go on finding fault with him anymore," I said. "He's learned his lesson, you can be sure of that."

"Lars," said Dessi, "tomorrow we'll go to Möja Sound."

"All right, let's," I said.

CHAPTER ELEVEN

WE DIDN'T MAKE for Möja Sound, though, for we were invited to have buns and fruit drinks at the naval officer's cottage. His name was Persson, the same as the cat's. He had an awfully nice wife. They came from Stockholm and only lived in their cottage during the summer holidays. The child, Ingalill, wasn't as peevish as we had thought before we became better acquainted, though of course she was very spoiled. After lunch Knut and I helped her father to put out a long line, and then we went to get our tent so as to set it up on the shore.

When we got to *Rudolfina*, the girls were just fishing something out of the sea with a net.

"A bottle!" I exclaimed.

Knut winced. He didn't want to hear anything more about bottles that day.

"A bottle message," said Rosalind, holding it up to the light. "Look, it's corked up and there's a paper inside. There is, I tell you!"

"Oh, how thrilling!" said Mirre. "Can it be from a shipwrecked vessel, do you think?"

We uncorked it and took out the paper. The letter

didn't look much the worse for wear and the writing was perfectly legible.

"OLD LADY IN DISTRESS ON LOKÖ REQUIRES IMMEDIATE ASSISTANCE," I read aloud. "It's dated, too—but just look here! It's been written today."

"Then perhaps we're still in time," said Rosalind.

"We'll have to go there, of course, and help her," said Knut.

"Do you think it's some trick?" asked Dessi.

"I expect she's without any food," said Mirre.

"Or else she's fallen and broken her leg," said Rosalind.

"Or got appendicitis," Knut suggested.

"It may be a joke or it may be genuine," I said, "but obviously we'll have to go and find out for ourselves." Everyone agreed.

"It's dead calm," said Dessi, "but we'll start up the engine, of course."

"Of course," I agreed, and started filling the blowlamp. Dessi looked at the chart. "Lokö, Lokö," she said, searching. "Wait, here we are. It lies north of Möja. How in the wide world did this bottle get here in one day? Especially in this flat calm."

"Perhaps there's a current the whole way," said Mirre.

"Anyhow, we can't let the old woman lie there and starve to death with her broken leg and appendicitis or whatever it is," said I.

"Have we fuel enough?" asked Dessi.

"Yes, the tank's more than half full," I replied.

Just then Captain Persson came rowing up. "Hullo, thinking of going already?" he asked.

"Shall we tell him about it?" whispered Dessi to me.

"No. He'd rush off in his racer and rescue the old lady himself. After all, we were the ones to find the bottle.— Yes," I called down to him, "we've got to get off, and we're in a bit of a hurry."

"Remember me to Kalle Hamper," he said. "And if you see a red cottage with a blue porch, and a boathouse that looks as if it were about to collapse on its haunches, go in and give them my kind regards too; you'll have a very pleasant time."

"But where is this cottage, then?" asked Rosalind.

"You'll find it all right, for yourselves," he said, laughing. "Good-bye, and a pleasant trip."

"He's nice, but he does say odd things," I remarked, and the others agreed with me. And when the ignition bulb glowed like a giant's eye, I started her up.

We stonka'd northward along the western side of Mö-ja. It was getting on toward six when we reached Lokö.

"Why, it's uninhabited," exclaimed Rosalind, for at first we couldn't see any houses, only birch and alder trees and some low bushes.

"All the worse for the old lady if she's hurt herself and has had to spend the night out of doors," said Dessi in troubled tones.

"Shall we land and reconnoiter?" said Knut.

But Dessi thought we ought to go chuffing round the

island first and look out for any signs of life. And then we noticed that it was cultivated. There were garden plots of sorts on all the southern slopes—lots and lots of them.

"Strawberries!" shouted Mirre. "There are strawberry plants everywhere. Look! It's absolutely stiff with strawberries. It's quite red!"

Then we realized that we had come to one of the strawberry islands.

"We must buy a few," said Rosalind. "They'll be cheap enough here."

"A few? You mean a whole lot," said Knut.

"Can we afford it?" asked Dessi and Mirre, who managed the housekeeping money.

"Oh, well, why not?" said Dessi. "Though perhaps not as many as we should like. But first we must go at once and look for the old lady."

"There's a jetty," I said. "I think we can lie alongside it; it looks quite deep."

We put in and Knut jumped ashore and made fast to some old posts that looked pretty rotten. Rotten too was the crooked old shed on the shore. There was a stack of packing cases by the wall and it looked a bit untidy down there. But Dessi thought it was beautiful. Sometimes she sees beauty where nobody else can.

"Now we'll spread out all over the island and look for the old lady," she said. "But remember one thing. None of us is so much as to touch a strawberry, do you hear? If we see anyone around we'll ask if we can buy some."

"Strawberries, strawberries," sang Pysen. He ought to

have gone to bed long since, but he was wide awake and we couldn't leave him alone in the boat, and none of us wanted to stay and look after him. We all wanted to look for the old lady in distress. The island wasn't so very big; we were bound to find her before long.

Rosalind and I followed a long track leading from the jetty. The cow parsley growing there was almost as tall as we were.

"Look," said she, "there's a house. I bet that's where she lives." It was a longish, red building with a roof that sagged in the middle. A black and white cat was sitting in the porch licking its back.

"Why, look, Lars," said Rosalind again, "the porch is blue. And the cottage is red. Do you think this is the place Captain Persson meant?"

"How was he to know we should find it? We never said where we were going. The archipelago's full of red houses with blue porches."

"But the shed by the jetty," said Rosalind.

The shed! It was certainly a boat shed, and one might say with truth that it was already subsiding onto its haunches, it was so aslant.

"Do you know, I'm beginning to have an idea," I said. "The message in the bottle . . ." Rosalind looked at me and nodded.

"It seems very mysterious," she said.

"Well, we'll go in, anyhow, because we've got to deliver the message from him. But wait, I'll call the others first."

We whistled our usual signal and they bobbed up from all sides. We told them about everything.

"Captain Persson was pulling our leg," said Dessi. "Of course he arranged the bottle message and put it where we were bound to find it. I do wonder just what we shall discover in that cottage."

"Well, obviously we shall know when we've gone in," said Mirre, stalking up to the cottage, holding Pysen's hand.

We followed. She knocked at the blue door.

"Yes? Come in," said somebody.

Mirre opened the door. There was a woman standing at a stove, stirring something in a pot. She was old and gray-haired.

"Dear heart alive!" she cried, her face lighting up. "Well, I never. You can always trust the captain. One, two, three, four, five of them," she said, counting us. "Five and a half," she added, catching sight of Pysen. "Perhaps we shall be able to manage. Perhaps you're in time. I'll just feed the pig first and then I'll come along."

We looked at each other. What were we going to be in time for?

"Captain Persson sent his kind regards," said Dessi.

"Thank you," said the old woman. "I understand. He is a nice gentleman and he shall have a few extra boxes of strawberries for this when I can find someone going in that direction."

We were rather bewildered and looked at one another again.

"We got a bottle message," began Mirre. "It said something about an old lady in distress here on Lokö, so we came to see if we could help."

"Don't bother to explain," I whispered.

The old woman put the swill into a bucket and pushed the stove rings into place.

"Yes, well, I don't know anything about a bottle message," she said. "But I told the captain I'd have to get all my berries picked and sent off to Stockholm by the steamer, and it goes tomorrow, early, at five in the morning, from Långviksnäs, and my daughter and a friend who generally come here for the picking were prevented from coming. If I don't get pickers soon the berries will all be overripe; they're on the verge of it already. So though it was a bit silly, that about the old lady, you might say that I am in distress, all the same. I'm beginning to find the picking too much for me, you see. I'm old and I turn giddy when I bend down."

"We'll pick, we'd love to; it would be fun," we cried.

Mirre took the bucket from her. "I can give this to the pig. Where is it?" she said. The old woman showed her the sty. And then she brought big bundles of cardboard pieces and showed us how to fold them into boxes, and while Dessi tucked Pysen up on a sofa, the rest of us fetched packing cases from the jetty. Then the old woman came and told us where to pick and how full to fill the boxes.

"And afterward you may eat as many as you like," she said, "but only one or two while you are picking, other-

wise we'll never be ready. Remember, we must hurry, and mind you don't trample the plants. Don't put in any unripe berries or ones that have had slugs on them."

And we picked. We went over the ground like an absolute berry-picking machine. And when we grew more accustomed to it we took less time to fill a box. Mirre was the quickest, but Rosalind ran her a close second. The big rosy berries were still warm from the sun, and smelled sweeter than jasmine, Dessi said.

On one of the plots the evening sun shone through two alders and seemed to paint a wide pathway of fiery red, shining strawberries. There was more fruit than leaves on the plants. I had never seen anything like it.

"You could really sit and eat straight off the ground," said Rosalind. "It only needs a little whipped cream and a spoon." Now and then we popped a berry into our mouths, but otherwise we just picked in silence, carrying boxes to the crates and fetching new supplies of cardboard. The sun sank down behind the pinewood on the other side of the water. We worked, racing against the failing daylight, moving from row to row, from plot to plot. It was the ripest berries that we ate, they tasted sweet and summery. The others, the dry, firm ones, that gave a sort of little creak between our fingers, we laid conscientiously in the cartons.

The old woman brought out a basket with buttermilk and coffee and great chunks of bread and butter with smoked pork on them.

"You're getting on fine," she said delightedly, spreading the cups on a smooth rock. "You're doing first class, with your nimble fingers. I used to be able to when I was young, but I make a poor showing now."

We straightened our backs and lay on our tummies round the basket and ate and ate and drank and drank. But we couldn't afford to waste time eating. We hurried back and started picking once more. The sun disappeared. It began to grow dark and it wasn't easy to see when we picked unripe berries. The mosquitoes sang round our ears, grasshoppers chirped, and out in the reeds a belated pike was jumping. But we picked on. My tummy was bulging with food and strawberries, my hands were as red as Mama's when she makes raspberry juice.

"How many boxes have you got left? Do you think we'll be able to finish? Nice of that Captain Persson, wasn't it?" was all we said to each other. I picked the last berries by the light of a pocket flashlight. There were two small plots left unpicked, but the old woman told us to leave them. It was half past eleven. We carried everything down to the jetty and helped the old lady nail down the lids of the crates. She was pleased with us and said we were really good. And if we couldn't eat any more that evening, we could do so next morning instead.

"Thank you; we'd rather wait till tomorrow morning," we replied, stroking our full tummies, which felt like drums.

Then Dessi went up to the cottage and stayed the night there so that Pysen wouldn't be scared when he woke and didn't know where he was. But Knut and I went farther along the island and collected worms, for we wanted to get up early and go fishing. It was a fine spot for worms. They lay looking like small shiny cords on the dewy grass as we shone the flashlight on them. One had to be silent as a fish and quick as a mongoose to get them before they snapped back into their holes again, leaving one with a handful of grass stems instead.

"I think we've got enough now," I said at last, yawning and stretching my back, which was stiff after all the picking. Then we heard an awful scream from down by the jetty. It was Mirre's voice.

We dashed down so fast that we upset half the worms out of the can. Mirre was hopping about on the cabin roof, shouting and waving her arms.

"Where did it go? Yes, Rosalind, I *know it was* a rat! Boys, we've got rats on board! In my bunk! Oh, can't Persson catch them? Call the cat, the cat, Rosalind, I tell you! Where's Persson? Puss, puss, kitty, good little Persson, come along."

"A rat?" I said. "You're making as much fuss as if your life was in danger! Where is this precious rat?"

"In my sleeping bag!" screamed Mirre. "If you'd had one in yours perhaps you'd know what it feels like to put your foot down and touch one of the beastly things. Oooh! Ugh! I shan't go into the cabin again until we've gotten rid of them."

But another voice issued from the cabin.

"Ohohoho! Oh, of all the sweetest, most adorable . . . Oh, quick, everybody, come in and have a look at Mirre's rats!"

Of course we went in. Rosalind was sitting on Mirre's bunk shaking with laughter.

"Persson, you sly little wretch—there!" she said. The kerosene lamp was alight, its rays falling on the sleeping bag. There lay three small kittens, crawling over each other. Persson stood beside them, her front paws on the bunk, her hind legs on the floor, lanky, unkempt, and thin as a lath, looking uneasy.

Mirre approached and joined Rosalind in worshiping the new family. She was slightly ashamed. Not so much

at having mistaken them for rats as for not having realized long before, from Persson's behavior, how matters
stood.

"They aren't just newly born," said Rosalind, for she
knows more about animals than the rest of us. "Obviously poor Persson must already have had them that
night when she had been out and came swimming back
and crept in and hid herself. This is the loveliest thing
that's happened yet on the whole trip. Just think how
delighted Pysen will be!"

"That was why Persson was so frantic to get aboard,
then," said I.

Persson jumped up into the bunk and lay like a pro-
tecting little wall round her children and started licking
them. They nuzzled about to find their food and then
began sucking and pounding. Persson looked proudly up
at us. Then she shut her eyes and started to purr.

"Well, now Dessi's responsible for three more members of the crew," I said.

CHAPTER TWELVE

I WAS AWAKENED by a motorboat arriving at the jetty. It was a neighbor from one of the adjacent islands who always took the old woman's strawberries when he went out to the steamer with Baltic herrings. Knut and I hurriedly put on our trousers and ran out. The old woman was there already, stacking her cases, and we helped put them aboard. Then we rowed out to a good feeding ground for perch that she showed us. We caught enough for a meal and some to spare.

Of course Pysen and Dessi were delighted with the kittens. He ignored both the duck and duckling. Now it was kittens and only kittens for him. He made a bed for them in the basket where he had had Persson and was much perturbed that Persson didn't approve of the arrangement, but persisted in carrying them away again.

"You mustn't bite your puppies," he said reprovingly when Persson took them by the back of the neck.

Mirre's sleeping bag in the darkest corner of the cabin was the only place, Persson considered, and from then on Mirre slept on a sail with an old coat over her, and said it was just as good. She was so thankful the kittens weren't rats that she would have managed without any covering at all if it had been necessary.

The old woman wanted to pay us for picking. We discussed the matter but decided not to accept any payment. We had been just picking for fun, and besides, she had turned us loose in the two remaining plots to eat as much as we wanted. But we weren't able to eat as many as we had expected. Strawberries are fairly substantial. Only Pysen ate, and he ate enough for two. We realized also that to a great extent the old woman had to live on the income from the plots and scrape together enough money during the short berry season to last her all the year, as Dessi said. She didn't need very much. She got potatoes from her own garden and fish from the sea, and a neighbor, the one who fetched the crates, would now and then put out a net for her. She had a cow and some hens, and felt she lived very well indeed. But Dessi told us that she must need every öre she could lay her hands on. Besides, we hadn't gone there to earn money but to help a lady in distress. Even Knut said that.

So we shook hands with her and picked the last plot clean, and went over the others and picked the berries we had overlooked. And when we left Lokö we had with us sixteen boxes of strawberries and a basket of eggs for a grocer in Långvik, and a message from the old lady, asking him to send her sugar and flour and a bottle of boracic lotion as soon as he could get in touch with somebody who was going Lokö way.

We beat upwind with some difficulty to get to Lång-vik. In the grocery store we called home and told them all that had happened since the last time we had done so. Mirre asked to speak to Aunt Bella, and said seriously, "I must tell you that we have had an addition to the family, aboard. You've become a grandmother, Aunt Bella."

The line wasn't very good, so she shouted as loudly as she could. The grocer looked up and stared, first at her, then at Dessi. And two summer visitors, in sunsuits, were there, and they stared as well.

"Yes, it's quite true," shouted Mirre. "Aren't you pleased? Do you realize who it is? Persson, of course; yes, that's right, Persson. Three days ago. On board, of course. They are so sweet, and they've got my sleeping bag, so they're quite comfortable. Good-bye, then, Aunt Bella; we'll call again soon."

Then we bought smoked sausage and pork and rye bread and buns. Then the shopkeeper said, "Don't you want anything else? For . . . for the invalid cousin? Some chocolate, perhaps, or a bottle of orange juice, or some cookies."

"Cousin?" we said, puzzled, not understanding what he meant. "What sick cousin?"

"Excuse me, but one can't help overhearing a conversation sometimes, without meaning to. And I heard that . . . well, that a little one had been born, on a boat, so I thought the mother might . . ." And the summer visitors stared at us most inquisitively.

"Oh, I must sit down!" gasped Mirre, turning to us. "Help me, or I shall pass out. He thinks it's a baby we had aboard *Rudolfina*."

When we could stop laughing we explained what it was about. When the shopkeeper heard that Persson was a cat belonging to Aunt Bella, he was as tickled as we were over the mistake, and the visitors laughed until one of them groaned and said, "I shall be ill! It's the funniest thing I ever heard."

"I thought you had a cousin who had had a baby, because you said your aunt had become a grandmother," said the shopkeeper.

"But I explained that it was Persson," said Mirre.

"Yes, but I thought you meant someone called Persson was the father."

"No," we said, "it's the mother who is called Persson."

"Who could understand that?" he said. "It is generally men who are called that."

"Oh!" said one of the visitors, laughing again until she was bent double.

Just as we were going, one of the other visitors said, "Don't you think the little mother ought to have something nice, even though she's only a cat?"

We hadn't thought of that. "Of course she ought to," we said, and asked for an ice, but they didn't have any.

"Persson likes butterscotch," said Rosalind. "We'll take her a big bit, she'll be awfully pleased."

We bought a big piece. But one of the ladies said, "Does it eat sardines?" We said we didn't know because we had never tried giving it such expensive food. But she said that all cats loved sardines. She had had several cats, and she knew. They liked sardines in oil. And she bought a can and asked us to take it to Persson. And the other lady wanted to send a can of lobster, but the grocer didn't stock it. We thanked them and left before they should think of other offerings de luxe.

Persson devoured all the sardines and the oil at one go. Then she had a pain and wanted to go ashore, and as soon as she had returned she had to go back again.

"Thus we see the curse of civilization," observed Dessi. "I wonder if it isn't time for us to withdraw from summer visitors and sardines in oil and other forms of civilization and look for that uninhabited island very soon."

"Yes, let's—oh, let's!" we all cried.

"I suggest that first we have a look in Möja Sound and see if we can find *Dunkan*. If we can't we'll put right out and begin looking for our island."

We set out but there was a contrary wind very soon. "Hm," I said, "the wind's gone over to the southwest. That means heading into it as far as Möja Sound. Tacking the whole way. And actually *Rudolfina* isn't too good at tacking. Or else we'd have to use the engine. Shall we bother about doing that when we could have a gorgeous sail toward Lilla Nassa archipelago, for instance, with this wind?"

"Lilla Nassa," said Knut, "of course we'll go to Lilla Nassa. Haven't I been talking about Lilla Nassa the whole time?"

"All who vote for Lilla Nassa put up their hands," said Mirre, putting up her own. Rosalind was also for Lilla Nassa. Dessi agreed. She wasn't keen on tacking either. And we had no reason to waste oil unnecessarily. The reserve we had might be needed, and our money as well. And it really wasn't likely that Kalle Hamper was still where Captain Persson had run across him.

"It can't be helped," said Dessi. "Now we'll turn our backs on culture and begin our real sailing."

We turned away from leafy Möja and then had a beam wind and a slight following wind between Oxkobb and Saffransskär and out toward the sea.

The archipelago became more open, the islets more sheer, the rocks shone pink, yellow-white, and violet. The sea lay dark blue with here and there a pale green streak.

That told one there was a shoal there. In crevices in the rocks flowers were blooming that we recognized from our botany studies, lemon-yellow stonecrop, pinky-lilac thrift, and red sorrel.

"Rosalind," I said, "it's your turn to write up the log-book."

She said her head was so empty she couldn't think of anything to write about. They wanted me to write it always, but I thought it would be much better to have a mixed compote. Dessi wrote about colors and scents and flowers and what the scenery was like wherever we were and Mirre methodically wrote what we had for breakfast and dinner and how much we spent on milk and herrings. Knut wrote how many perch we had caught and how long we took on our way between different anchorages every night. He always looked at the time and made a note of when we anchored and when we hoisted the anchor. Rosalind and I had undertaken to describe all our adventures. But now she went on strike.

"My brain won't function in this heavenly weather," she said.

"Stir it up, then," I said. "Remember how you used to in the old days." I thought of a time a few years back. Rosalind had had some homework she couldn't manage. Papa was away. Mama and Dessi are no mathematicians. Mirre was muddling along with her own homework and I was a year behind Rosalind, so I couldn't help her. She disappeared. Later Mama went out into the hall. Rosalind was standing on her head in a corner, moaning.

"My dear child, what is the matter?" asked Mama, turning her right side up again.

Rosalind was red and breathless. She said, "I read about a clever Chinese who always used to stand on his head awhile whenever he had to think. He said it freshened up his brain." Then she went in and tackled her sums again. This time she got them right and was delighted. She had hit on a splendid way of solving her difficulties. She practiced this new method for the whole of the term. Usually it answered very well. But things would probably have turned out all right anyhow. They usually did, for Rosalind.

"It's too hot to stand on my head," she said. "Give me the wretched old logbook, then." She started writing.

"Read it out," I said when she had finished. She read:

"All of us sunburned. Lars has lost the skin off his nose, Knut's shoulders look like raw beef, the deck is littered with what looks like snow but is really flakes of skin from the peeling bodies of the young Peep-Larssons. In the wake are four gulls being fed with rusks by Flag Officer Larsson. A little way for'ard one duck and seven charming ducklings are swimming landward. In the cabin is one cat with three puppies."

"You said puppies!" cried Pysen triumphantly. "They are called *kittens*—didn't you know?" For now that he knew he would never say it wrong.

"In Långvik I came across some dogs," continued Rosalind, "a prize-winning English setter, Flight, and a mongrel with beautiful eyes and a very curly tail."

"Can't you think of any more animals?" I inquired.

She pondered a little, then went on writing.

"Well?" I asked.

"On the cabin roof are about a hundred mosquito corpses and a dead spider," she read. "Persson seems to have picked up some ticks in the woods, for she keeps scratching. Rosalind feels like a sleepy sloth. The others are a collection of Cheshire cats, smiling at the sun."

Then she threw the book at me and stretched out on her stomach on the seat in the well.

"Heavenly!" she said. "Nobody can be having such a gorgeous time as we are."

We sucked lemon drops and drank lemonade. Persson took a little time off from her maternal duties and came up and sunned herself on deck. Rosalind got hold of her and hunted for the tick until she caught it.

"The wind's freshening," said Dessi presently. "You'll see, soon it will be blowing hard. Do you think we ought to reef a bit before going farther out, Lars?"

Knut stuck out his underlip discontentedly.

"Shorten sail now, just when we're going so marvelously?"

I wasn't keen on doing so, but I let Dessi have her own way, chiefly for Pysen's sake. And soon afterward I was glad I had done so. For when we reached Vitharorna the wind had become very strong indeed.

"Perhaps we oughtn't to go out so far in a little boat like this," I said, feeling slightly uneasy.

"We're halfway to Lilla Nassa," said Dessi. "If we turn

back we'll have to beat upwind. But with the wind in this quarter it will take us right into the harbor there."

"But we'll have to get back again as well," I said.

"We're in no hurry; we can stay there till the wind changes," said Knut.

The foam dashed up. There was salt on our lips and our faces felt stiff with spray. Pysen, who was lying asleep, rolled out of his bunk when a gust of wind took the boat. Mirre sat on the floor in the cabin and took him on her lap, where he went on sleeping.

"Squally!" shouted Knut delightedly.

"We ought to have shortened sail still more," I said.

The sea birds shrieked. It sounded unusually piercing and high. The waves reared themselves steeply, with green-white foam on their crests. They no longer clucked and rippled against Rudolfina's sides. They struck at her with a violence that made the whole hull shudder. Rosalind's wet curls hung over her eyes in wisps, and Dessi's sunglasses blew into the sea.

"Come down!" I shouted to Knut, who was messing around on deck. "Come down before you fall overboard again. We couldn't get you out this time."

Astern of us was the dinghy, high on the summit of a wave, and it looked as though we were yards below it. It was a horrid feeling.

Knut came stumbling down. "I can see Lilla Nassa now," he said.

In the cabin, knapsacks and packets of biscuits were rolling around, and our oilskins and shore-going clothes swung wildly on their pegs. Dessi got the life belts and put one on the protesting Knut.

"In a sea like this, one wouldn't manage to keep afloat long just by swimming," she said.

Bottles of lemonade rolled around in the hold and the Peep saucepan leapt out of its container and landed on the floor. Pysen whimpered and stirred on Mirre's knee, but didn't wake. I stood straddled in the steering well, being flung against the edge when the waves struck the boat. My fingers were cramped from clinging to the helm. We had the wind broadside on, and the waves also, so I tacked a bit and headed for the Björkskär archipelago. That eased her slightly, but the speed slackened too and we wallowed continually in the trough of the waves. The bay lies open right down to Sandhamn, and the waves had time to pile mountainously before they reached us.

If it doesn't improve soon, we'll have to turn back anyhow, I thought. Then I saw that Lilla Nassa lay abaft the beam already, on our port quarter, as Knut said, having learned the term from his sea stories.

"We're O.K. now," I cried as we made for the lee of the group of islands, for as soon as we got the wind astern, a great calm fell over Rudolfina. The wind seemed to have died down, though it hadn't really done so, and long waves swung us along, gently and friendly. Before many minutes we were passing Prästkobb and could see the approach to Lilla Nassa bay, between Västerskär and

Rönnkobb. I edged in closer to Rönnkobb. But that I ought never to have done.

Bummelibummelibummelibum! Rudolfina struck an underwater obstruction, glided over it, then over another and still another. She slithered over them as if they had been greased hogs' backs. The thought flashed through my mind, "Is this why it's called Lilla Nassa* and are these the little pigs whose acquaintance we are making?" Our boat was lifted, then sank, was lifted, then sank again. We staggered under the shocks, unable to say more than "What . . ." all together before it was over.

"Dessi! Look out!" I yelled. But both Dessi and Rosalind had rushed for'ard and were signaling wildly to me to bear closer to Västerskär instead. Of course I did so. Another slight, very slight jar and we were clear. Then in we flew at speed, and luffed smartly in the lee of Rönnkobb, gliding into a little harbor basin with smooth, polished slabs of rock and a small cement jetty. Higher up we saw a couple of little fishing shacks.

"Whew!" I said, wiping the cold sweat from my forehead. "That wasn't shown on the chart. It was awful!"

"If *Rudolfina* had been one of those thin mahogany shells, we'd have been smashed to smithereens," screamed Knut.

"If we drew a few inches more we'd have gone aground," said Rosalind.

In the harbor the water lay smooth as a floor. A num-

* *Lilla Nassa*—"little piglet" in Swedish.

ber of swallows flew up from the eaves of the roof of the larger of the two huts and circled anxiously around as we glided toward the jetty.

"Weren't you frightened, Lars?" asked Rosalind.

"Shut up! Put out the fenders instead of jabbering," I said. "Give a thought to the planking, can't you?"

"The boy's as bad as the dye manager, or worse," said Knut.

I realized it myself, but one is apt to be a bit short-tempered sometimes when one has been thoroughly scared.

Pysen wakened and sat up. "Oh, look," he said, "are we in a different country?"

"Yes, quite different," said Dessi.

"Not a strawberry one," said Pysen.

No, anything less like a strawberry plot could scarcely be imagined. Smooth, bare rocks, some of them rather sheer, no trees, scarcely any bushes, only one or two tufts of scrubby marram grass.

"Surely nobody lives in those cottages," said Dessi.

"If they did they'd have a boat here," I said. "Probably it's just a couple of fishing shacks for the Möja people. This island's called Sprickopp.* That's because the inlet cuts deep into the rock. But the person responsible for that chart can't ever have been here. I hope he does come soon and tries to put in alongside Rönnkobb."

Rosalind was first ashore. She had managed to make a tour of inspection around the shacks before the rest of us

* "Rip-up."

had gotten ourselves sorted out. She came running back.

"There's not a soul to be seen and the sheds are locked. Don't let Persson come ashore without a leash. There are birds all over the place, and some of them are breeding."

We went up and looked around. It was thick, thick with swallows' nests under the eaves of the roof of the larger shed. The young swallows were just learning to fly, and there was a fluttering and babbling, frightened little heads disappearing into their holes whenever we approached, and anxious parents circling around our ears, begging us to go away again. The rocks were covered with sea birds that flapped up noisily before we could get near them.

"We must be careful," said Dessi. "We mustn't disturb them too much. This is their island and they look on us as invaders."

She and I went up to the stone cairn on the highest outcrop of rock and looked out over the skerries of Lilla Nassa.

"There's a whole archipelago of rocks and islands," she said, "I'd like to stay here for a bit. It's all so clean and beautiful."

"Well, I don't know about clean," I said, looking at the bird droppings on the rocks, and eggshells, fishbones, and feathers in the crannies.

"Clean, beautiful lines," said Dessi. "No scratches or scribbles. No people. So peaceful and far away from everything."

"We may have to stay here," I replied, "because it looks like bad weather. So you may find you will have too much of it."

The sea beyond was like a boiling pot. It boomed and thundered and every time a wave struck the rocks it flung clouds of spray far up the cliff face. But in the shallows between the islets the water was wonderfully smooth and still.

We swam, diving in from the rocks, all except Pysen. The water was much colder out there. Pysen let the duck and duckling swim in rock pools. The water was warmer there. Of course he wanted the kittens to try and swim too, but luckily Mirre prevented that.

But it became more and more overcast, and dark,

swollen clouds spread in an angry flock across the sky. Then came thunder and lightning and torrents of rain. We hastily took shelter in *Rudolfina*, crowded into the cabin, and ate a hurriedly prepared scratch meal, while the rain pattered on the cabin roof and dripped down the backs of our necks from the edge of the skylight. Lightning flashed here and there and thunder echoes rolled around the rocks.

"Suppose the mast is struck by lightning!" said Knut.

But I nudged his arm so that he shouldn't frighten the girls. Mirre was already a bit white about the gills. She is no fonder of lightning than she is of rats.

There was no question of putting up the tent in such weather, and besides, there was no convenient spot. So we all slept aboard. The rain was slackening. I baled out the boat before turning in. That she should have shipped a certain amount of water under the sails and from the general downpour was not surprising—after all, we didn't have a self-bailing well—but I hadn't expected to have to keep on pumping for so long.

"*Tanja III* never shipped as much water as this," I said.

"Well, you'd better go back to her, then," said Knut.

"Kindly do some pumping yourself, since you enjoy it," I said.

But he started brushing his teeth in a great hurry, gargling as though he had tonsillitis, and by the time he had finished I had done the pumping, which of course was what he had been counting on.

"Ha! Ha! hissed the villain," he said, and scuttled off out of the way of my wrath.

"It's Sunday tomorrow," I said to Mirre, "and those of us who have been sailing before the mast should have their chocolate brought them in bed. Full mugs and lots of buns."

"Not if you get up at five to go fishing," she said. "You'll have to shift for yourselves in that case."

"I don't think this is a good place for perch," I said, "so I thought I'd take it easy and stay in bed till nine."

Then I scrapped with Knut a bit. It was his turn to lie on the sail bag, but when I came into the fo'c'sle I found he had already taken possession of the bunk.

"First come first served," he said.

"Kindly get served elsewhere," I said, and I took hold of his legs and hauled him out.

"That old sack's as hard as nails; it's much more suitable for you," he rejoined.

"What's the fight about?" called Rosalind. "May we join in?" And she threw an old oilskin coat at us. It wasn't very dry; she had just been wearing it to take Persson ashore for an evening walk. But she got it back, and a pair of soaking wet rubber boots into the bargain.

"Pipe down a bit," said Dessi, shushing us. "Don't wake Pysen."

"Nor Persson and the kittens neither, noho!" said Pysen.

He had slept so much during the day that he was wide awake. He wanted to throw shoes around, too. Dessi, who always tried to be fair, said he might throw two shoes and that would be enough. So he threw one at Rosalind, then climbed down and came behind the mast and threw the other at Knut's behind. Then he went back to bed. But since he couldn't sleep, he sang ballads to us. They sounded like this:

One kitty shall ride in Fimbo
When it gets its eyes,
And the other shall ride in Lyxen,
And lots and lots of kittens shall ride in another car
That Lars will buy at Woolworth's;
And Persson shall ride in a huge big motorcar.
Papa will buy one

And I shall ride in a real car
And nobody else shall ride in it
Only Lars and me
And Knut.
Noho, not Knut.
Yes, he shall come too
And we will buy ices
And eat them in the car.
And Persson shall have an ice
And the kittens shall have a taste
When they get eyes.
Mirre said they should.
And Persson has got eyes
But the kittens haven't
And we mustn't poke them
Because it hurts them if we do
And I can swim and I can swim and I can swim
And I shall be big soon
And swim, swim, swim . . .

CHAPTER THIRTEEN

I FELL ASLEEP while Pysen was droning his melody all on one note. Some hours later I was awakened by another voice which yelled and shouted. It was Knut.

"I'm lying in the water! We're sinking! Help! We're going down, we're on the bottom! Get up!"

I got up. Splash! went the floorboards when I set foot on them. Smack! sounded as Knut and I banged our heads together.

"Oh!" cried Rosalind from the cabin. "It's full of water in here, get up all of you, quickly. Mirre, wake up!"

Knut pushed back the cabin roof. He climbed out and I followed. I peered over the gunwale. *Rudolfina* lay unpleasantly deep in the water.

Up came Dessi and Rosalind and Pysen, with all the cats, and finally Mirre tumbled out of the cabin.

"Pump! Pump, everybody, we must all pump together!" shouted Rosalind.

Mirre started pumping, but I seized a bucket, pushed back the cabin roof again, and went down and began handing up buckets of water to Dessi, who took them from me and emptied them into the sea. Pumping by itself wouldn't do much good.

"This can't be from the rain," I said. "I thought there was an awful lot of water last night when I pumped. We must have sprung a leak. It must have happened when we scraped over those rocks just outside here, of course."

The floorboards were awash. Bottles of lemonade were floating around. Two packets of rye crackers, three sea-boots, an oilskin, and Mirre's pink petticoat had fallen into the water.

Rosalind came along with another bucket, and we baled. Sometimes in our hurry we knocked the buckets against the side so that half the water tipped out and splashed over us. Dessi and Knut did the emptying. Mirre worked away at the pump.

"It's getting less, it's improving by degrees," I said.

It certainly was, but it took some time before *Rudolfina* was at last pumped dry.

"Do you really mean there's a hole in the ship's bottom?" said Mirre as we panted for breath.

"Obviously," answered Rosalind and Knut.

"What else could it be?" I asked. We stood there shivering in the pale morning light. It was only just after half past five. The sky was overcast. The rain had stopped, but out at sea we could hear the waves roaring.

"You can all go and lie down in peace," I said. "I'll keep watch and pump again if need be."

"I'll stay with you," said Dessi. "Go and lie down, you others."

They protested.

"Go and lie down in such a rat trap?" said Knut.

Rosalind said, "Wouldn't it be better to find out where the leak is?"

"Of course, but I don't suppose we can mend it," I said.

"No; *Rudolfina* will have to go to a repair yard," said Dessi with a sigh. "Think what it will cost! And how shall we manage to get her there?"

"We'll manage somehow," I said, though I was far from sure of it.

"Anyway, none of us can sleep at the moment," said Rosalind.

I began searching the bottom of the boat to try and find the place where the water was coming in. We lifted up the floorboards and peered in under the engine, going on into the cabin and stacking all the lemonade bottles on deck so as to be able to see. We found no hole anywhere, but it was quite evident that there was one somewhere, for water was beginning to seep through into the hold again. Not until I had reached the fo'c'sle and gotten rid of all the clutter there did I manage to find what was wrong.

"There it is!" shouted Rosalind, who was leaning over my shoulder. "That's where it's trickling in."

"Yes, that's it," I replied. "Be a dear and fetch a flashlight."

The starboard strake had obviously sprung. The thick oak plank bulged slightly inward at one place and the Baltic was seeping slowly but surely through the crack.

"And I thought we had skidded over the pig's backs so

splendidly," I said. "There must have been a sharp point on one of those hidden rocks."

"How shall we manage to plug it?" said Dessi.

"The dye manager used to caulk *Tanja III* with plastellina," said Mirre.

"It wouldn't be any good in this case," I said. "Besides, *Tanja* hadn't any cracks, she was only a tiny bit open at the seams in spring, before she'd been in the water long enough for the mahogany to swell. Plastellina's all very well in a case like that, but this is quite another kettle of fish."

"Well, then, what?"

"I think *Rudolfina* needs slipping and being properly attended to," I said gloomily. "She'll have to have a new plank put in instead of that damaged one. But we can't manage that now, of course."

"But supposing we could putty up the hole temporarily," said Dessi, "do you think there would be any risk in going out in her then?"

"If we struck a rock again that crack might open up altogether and the boat would fill with water before we could say knife. It would be no good pumping or baling then; we should just go down," I said.

"A heavy sea would probably force in that damaged plank," said Rosalind. "But we must think of something. Look how it's coming through!"

Knut said, "Perhaps I could lie on the hole and stop it up. I read about a boy in Holland who saw a hole in the dike, and he thrust his arm in and stayed there until people came and mended it, and he saved the whole town from being flooded."

"I've never believed that story," I said. "Besides, I don't think you are heavy or thick enough to stop up the leak. We'll have to patch it up in some other way."

We got out the toolbox, but there wasn't anything in it that was helpful in the circumstances. Hammer, pincers, screwdriver, brace and bit, a little saw, copper nails, screws, steel wire, some old fittings, and a crowbar that I used sometimes when the flywheel wouldn't budge to get it to move. I pondered awhile, pumping in the meantime.

"If I had a tough, substantial bit of wood about that size," I said, "I should try and nail it on so that it held the plank together and prevented it from opening. Say, how about looking for one on the island? There's sure to be some wood around somewhere. Perhaps some boards or something may have been washed ashore."

We scattered and searched the whole of Sprickopp. But the only wood we found was a little pile of alder sticks near the larger shed, and they were of no use whatever. Rosalind and Mirre took the dinghy and rowed across to the skerries close by, but the small amount of wood they found there was as white and thin as paper, and wouldn't have held any nails.

"I know," said Mirre. "How big has it got to be?"

"About so big," I said, demonstrating.

"Well, we can use the chopping board, then; there's no need to look further."

The board was exactly the right size. It was a fairly large one of birchwood, about an inch thick.

Then I set to work. First I knocked the strained plank back with the crowbar and got it slightly more into place. Then I bored six small holes in the chopping board and drove screws through them and into the plank. Nails would not have held. Then I made little wedges of alder wood, and plugged the places where the board didn't quite fit the plank.

"It's helping," said Dessi, "you can see that it helps. Hardly any water's coming through now."

"Well, it's not very firm, but it feels a bit more secure. And now, if there's any plastellina I'd be glad if you could find it, Mirre, please."

"I'm ashamed to say we never thought of bringing any," said she.

"Wouldn't red lead and tow do just as well?" asked Dessi. "Isn't that what they use in the dockyards?"

"Yes, of course, but we haven't any of that, either."

"It's still coming in a bit, but not nearly so much," said Knut, looking at it.

"We could make putty with chalk and linseed oil," I mused aloud. "We've got linseed oil actually, but where can we get chalk from?"

"Bird droppings," said Knut. "They look just like chalk and there are plenty here. Shall I go and scrape some off the rocks?"

Then Mirre rushed off and began looking for something in her big bathing bag.

"Wouldn't this do?" she asked. It was a box with six little sticks of children's modeling clay.

"Oh," screamed Pysen. "Is that some of my clay?"

"Yes," she said, "Mama put it in but she said I was to hide it until Pysen didn't know what to do with himself and got troublesome. But it can't be helped. Will it do as well as plastellina?"

"I don't know," I replied. "We can always try; it's very like it, anyhow."

But it was a complete failure.

"It won't work," I said. "It might if the wood weren't wet, perhaps. But look how stiff and unworkable it gets when the wet touches it. And it won't stick to the wood."

"Red lead and tow!" sighed Dessi again.

"What is tow?" asked Mirre. "Frayed rope, or what? Couldn't we unravel some rope? We've plenty of that."

"Yes, unravel some, it might do all right," I said, "but what could we soak it in?"

"Linseed oil," said Dessi.

"That wouldn't do. The wood would absorb it and the water would get through the tow anyway."

"Linseed oil and modeling clay mixed," said Rosalind.

"Well, we can try, anyhow," I said, "for we've got to do something."

We found a rope end that was already a bit frayed. We had lots of that, as we used to practice splicing. It was easy to unravel and we soon had quite a little pile. Then we took linseed oil and modeling clay and mixed that with the tow, kneading and pounding them with our fingers, rubbing them together until Dessi got her thumbs quite sore.

"Well, I think that's the best we can do," said Mirre at last.

"Just a bit more oil," I said. "There!"

We sat back on our heels in the narrow little fo'c'sle and did our best to plug up the leak. But I soon saw that I must undo all I had done up till now, take off the chopping board and fill up the cracks first, and then screw on the board again and push in the wedges. I said I had now realized that the crack would have to be stopped up from the outer side, and that couldn't be managed, since it was low down by the keel.

"Pooh!" said Rosalind. "Fancy talking like that! Just you listen to the Peep-Larsson water beast! Of course one can duck beneath the hull and push in a little tow. Don't do any more from the inside until I've seen if I can cope with that rotten board from outside."

"Wait," said Dessi, "I don't like the idea of your doing that."

"Excuse me, Captain, but this is where I mutiny," said Rosalind, and got hold of her bathing suit in the cabin. She then went up on deck and we heard the splash before we had time to put our heads through the fo'c'sle door.

We hung a rope straight from the crack in the fo'c'sle out of the skylight and down into the water to mark the place where the leak was. She had to go down three times before she found where the blow had struck *Ru-*

dolfina's spreading hull. But find it she did at last, and told us to hand down a little more tow.

"Come up," I said. "To start with, it's stopped coming in, now, and to go on with, we can pull the boat farther up onto the shore and get at the leak that way. Besides, we aren't fish, anyway."

"We know you are awfully good at staying under water," said Dessi, "but it can't be good for you to hold your breath for so long, time after time."

"Mind you don't get a gulp of cold water," said Knut.

But Mirre handed down a fistful of tow and said, "Let her do it, she'll be all right. You know how she's practiced being under water." And Rosalind drew a deep breath and ducked again.

When she came up I wanted to take over, but she wasn't having any. "It's best for me to go on because I know where to find it," she said. And she disappeared below the surface exactly like a seal diving for fish. She came up for air and disappeared once more. When she came up next time she said, "I give up. It's impossible to push the stuff in; it only comes out again."

"You did awfully well even though it may not have been any good," said Dessi.

But I said, "Now we'll haul *Rudolfina* up alongside the quay as far as we can. We must get the leak out of the water so that the hull can dry a bit before we try again."

We all pulled together. We got her bow up onto the shore, right out of the water, but not far enough. Then we thought of weighing down the stern, so we carried down a lot of stones. That helped. It did the trick. For each stone we put in made the stern sink lower and raised the level of the bow, and we were able to pull her a little bit higher, and still a little more. And at last the damaged plank appeared.

It was bad, but not as bad as we had feared. Mirre had evidently expected a great gaping hole, for she said, "Is it only as bad as that!" She sounded almost disappointed.

"It can be serious enough," said Dessi, "but I've an idea we can put it right."

"Now we'll let it dry for a bit," I said, "and meanwhile we'll have breakfast, because I'm hungry enough to eat a stone, provided it was lightly boiled."

"But now I haven't got any clay," said Pysen, suddenly becoming much aggrieved. "You've taken it all, and Mama said it was mine, yoho yes, she did."

Then Knut hit on the idea that he and Pysen should drag stones in Fimbo and Lyxen. Knut had picked up all the pretty little stones he had seen whenever he had landed. And now stone carrying went on, down *Rudolfina*'s sloping gangplank.

We hung up our soaked possessions to dry. The inside of the sail bag was dripping wet, rugs and sleeping bags were the same. We prepared chocolate, and donned slacks and woollies, for it was not exactly warm.

"I think it ought to be dry enough now for us to start plugging the leak properly," I said.

We worked the tow again, so as to get it really soft, and then started caulking in earnest. This time everything went well. I used a butter knife to push it in with, and shoved as hard as I could. It looked really tidy when it was done.

"We ought to have a chopping board on the outside, too, for safety's sake," I said, and started looking around again for pieces of wood. I debated whether to take the plaques on which the lantern brackets were fixed, but they were too small.

"We'll use a bit of the cabin floorboards," I said. "It's more important to mend the leak than to look smart." So I prised loose one of the floorboards and screwed it to the damaged one with a great many brass screws.

"Now there's nothing more we can do," I said.

We removed the stones and pushed *Rudolfina* back into the water. Then we went to see if the fo'c'sle was still leaking. But it was perfectly dry. Splendid! At last we could breathe freely, wander about on land, swim, and enjoy ourselves in spite of the weather.

So Rosalind and I went around the skerries and photographed birds and birds' nests. The loveliest bird we saw was a single Caspian tern which seemed to hover motionless in the air, looking down searching for fish. It remained there practically all day above a little shoal where there must have been fish spawn, only diving occasionally. It was so slim and dainty, and its snow-white underparts and bright-red beak gleamed against the sullen gray sky. We watched it from the boat; it was quite near but not a bit scared of us. We called it the Queen of Lilla Nassa, for not until some time later, when we got home and looked it up in our bird book, did we know what sort it was.

Pysen went around in his life jacket just the same when we were ashore. For the rocks were steep and slippery after the rain. But he was busy and happy, first over the stone carrying, and then with boats which we carved for him from bits of bark which had floated ashore. He had a whole fleet, which he sailed from one pool to another.

Dessi kept apart, by herself. She disappeared with her sketch book, beyond the two sheds, and we kept to the other side of them. Mirre had started the troublesome business of preparing pork dumplings. Every now and then I went aboard to make sure we were not shipping any water.

Knut wasn't very thrilled with Lilla Nassa after all.

"You can't find anything to do here," he said. "If one were a sportsman and could shoot birds, perhaps, but one can't and doesn't want to, anyhow. And it would be really fun to build a raft and sail round this lagoon in it, but there's nothing to build one with. And we can't make a cabin of spruce because there aren't any spruce firs. And the stones here don't amount to much."

I nearly added that there weren't any natives to trade with, either. But I thought he had heard enough about that old bit of silliness, so I only said that when one was stormbound there was nothing to do but to be patient.

The water inside the harbor basin looked rather strange. There weren't any waves there but it kept moving; there was a sort of swell, and it rose and fell just as if it were breathing.

"There's a giant outside the bay, sucking in the water and blowing it out again," said Rosalind. "And it was his nose that we struck that made the hole in our bottom. Look, there's a bit of his beard!" It was a great tangle of seaweed floating around the inlet.

I have always felt that Rosalind could think up quite as amusing stories as the ones Dessi sometimes tells us. But she won't do it. She starts something occasionally but it never comes to anything. She always wants to share in every possible adventure but I am the one who has to tell about them, and it is Dessi who concocts new ones when necessary. Rosalind is going to be a vet and marry a gamekeeper, or perhaps a forestry officer, she says. But before getting married she intends to swim the Kattegat and the English Channel. Because swimming is the thing she loves best, better even than fussing with animals.

The sea birds had grown used to us by now. The downy gull chicks, which at first had been kept back by their anxious parents, began swimming around occasionally on their own right in the harbor. In a grassy hollow a scoter was still brooding her eggs, and we could get up close to her with the camera without her flying off. Rosalind went around feeding all the birds on rye biscuit, for the packets that had become waterlogged were unfit for human consumption. In the end the scoter would take biscuit crumbs right out of her hand.

"If we stay here any longer the whole place will be like

a poultry farm," said Mirre, who wasn't very pleased, because the birds, once they had gotten over their shyness, would come aboard to beg for food, and left visiting cards all over *Rudolfina*. But Rosalind was only too glad to scrub the deck after her beloved friends. One day a dropping from a black-backed gull fell smack onto her bread and butter just as she was about to take a mouthful. But she only laughed and called to it, "Yes, you rascal, you thought out the only way of getting this for yourself!" And she broke it in pieces and threw it to the gull. Next moment there was an absolute swarm of them hovering over the boat, all anxious to get a bit.

It seemed as if the stormy weather wouldn't ever let up. On the third day there was sunshine, but the sea was rougher than ever, and to go out in *Rudolfina* was not to be thought of. In the morning we had lemonade instead of chocolate. There was no more water in the demijohn.

"It's beginning to get critical," said Dessi. "If only we had thought to put out a few buckets when it was raining."

"Lemonade is nice," said Knut, "but not first thing in the morning."

"I didn't know the demijohn was nearly empty," said Mirre. "I managed to get a drop to make some 'funny milk' for Pysen and Persson, but it won't last long."

"If only there were a well or spring," said Rosalind.

"We'd have been able to get water out of the rock puddles," said Mirre, "only they are full of feathers and rubbish and little creatures. We ought to have cleaned them out before the rain and used them instead of a well."

"Besides, Pysen has been around paddling in all of them," said Dessi, "so they wouldn't be very appetizing."

"Well, we'll be able to manage all right on lemonade for a couple more days," I said, "and we can use salt water for washing up and cooking potatoes and fish."

That evening we brushed our teeth in lemonade.

CHAPTER FOURTEEN

FOR ONE MORE DAY we were forced to remain where we were. But during the night I woke up because of the strange silence all around us. The thunder and roaring of the waves, to which we had become accustomed, had changed to a mild, sleepy hushing. At three o'clock I put out my head and looked up at the pennant. Yes, it was hanging limp and motionless. At six o'clock I roused the crew, for the morning breeze was getting up, a light westerly wind.

"We must get off," I said. "It might start blowing again, one can never tell, so it is better to take the opportunity now."

Then began a hunt for the gear we had taken ashore, Pysen's bark boats and ducks, our fishing rods, and Knut's stones. But we were as quick as we could be, and for safety's sake I set the engine going so that we shouldn't have difficulty in getting out of the flat calm in the inner haven, or perhaps drive against those wretched rocks again.

Gulls and terns followed us through the narrows, shrieking for their breakfast. But we didn't even have time to think of our own until we were out beyond

Rönnkobb again and felt a little safer. Then we set sail and stopped the engine.

"What a pity we daren't go out any farther this time," said Dessi. "One day I shall sail right out to sea as far as I can go and see what happens."

"You'll end up somewhere in Russia," said Mirre. "That's to say if you can manage on your own all that time. Or didn't you mean to be alone?"

"I don't know," she murmured.

"But where shall we go now?" I asked.

"Ought we to go to a repair yard and get that plank looked at?" said Dessi. "We needn't have anything done if it isn't necessary."

"It would be a long way to a repair yard," I said. "I think the nearest one is at Djurö. But we can go in that direction, anyway. And now let's have some sandwiches —what do you say?"

The remaining rye crackers had become soft and soggy from the damp on board and tasted insipid, but we ate them nevertheless, for the fresh bread was all finished. We washed them down with lemonade, which we drank with mixed feelings. Try drinking lemonade and only lemonade, day after day, and you'll know why! For my part I had determined never to go in for it much in the future.

"Go easy with it," said Mirre. "We've only three bottles left."

"Lilla Nassa's out of sight now, but look, how queer!" said Rosalind.

"It's snowing!" shouted Pysen. "Snowing into the sea! We'll throw snowballs, Lars!"

I turned around. Not only had Lilla Nassa disappeared, but the whole horizon also. It seemed wrapped in a soft, woolly white fleece. And that woolly thing came drifting after us, billowing in great soft clouds along the water.

"Fog!" I shouted. "We're in for a fog. How shall we find our way? Take the tiller, Dessi, we'll have to hurry as fast as we can. There's not much we can do with this little wind, but perhaps the engine will help."

The engine was still warm and started up unusually quickly.

"Now we need *Tanja's* spinnaker to help; it would get us to land in a twinkling," said Rosalind. This time Knut made no protest.

The fog closed in on us, but our sturdy old Bruzaholmer stonka'd on without faltering once, just as though it knew how serious the situation was.

"A race," said Knut. "I think the fog's going to win. Then of course we'll go aground again."

"The first possible harbor, eh, Lars?" said Dessi, studying the chart. I nodded.

"Yes, though we'll keep going as long as we can, of course. We can't risk being stuck without water again, perhaps for several days. And Mama is probably pretty worried already at not hearing from us for some time. We must get ashore and phone her."

"It's gaining on us," said Dessi, "though it seems to move very slowly."

"That's because it hasn't any engine to help it," said Knut. Vitharorna loomed up and glided past. Soon it was lost in the mist.

"We'll try and make Möja if we can," I said.

By the time we passed Roskär the fog had crept closer. Small fluffy white wisps detached themselves from the fleece and came drifting along ahead of it. The fleece spread out northward and southward and slowly and surely enfolded us in a downy covering. The sun was already dim and shone a pallid gold through the vapor. We had made our way, with difficulty, past Stortistronskär, when the damp white vapor trails began really enshrouding us.

"We shan't make Möja, but we may get as far as Saffransskär before it's so thick that we can't see a yard ahead," I said.

"Make for Saffransskär, then," said Dessi.

We reached it. Just as the fog belt was swallowing us up and all around us had turned milky white, Saffransskär opened its arms to us and took us to its breast.

It was like a miracle, I thought, as I stopped the engine.

From that frightening, blinding wet white mist, we floated into a different world. The sun shone. A cowbell tinkled. A mallard and her ducklings were swimming in the reeds. The shore was covered with red and gold flowers. Beyond the bay the mist drifted along in cloud after cloud, but it seemed exactly as if it couldn't find us. It had no power over this flowery island and had to give way.

"This'll do fine, under the rock here," I said, and at last dared to breathe freely.

"Let go the anchor!" shouted Dessi to Mirre. The anchor splashed and the cable rattled. When we had lowered the sail Mirre said, "There are cows here. There'll be water and a telephone, you'll see."

"Well, I'll row ashore and reconnoiter," said Knut.

"Yes, but there's to be no briefcase business," said Dessi.

"I never meant to take it," said Knut, reddening.

"Run along, then, but hurry, because we're all wanting to get ashore as soon as possible. You may as well take a bucket in case you manage to get hold of some water."

Knut took a can and climbed into the dinghy. Dessi and Mirre began busying themselves with food.

"We haven't many provisions left," said Dessi, scraping the butter tin. "We'll have to find a grocer's soon."

"The blessings of civilization," I said, laughing a little.

Mirre laid the biscuits out to dry on the cabin roof and said we wouldn't ever be so stupid as to take up space again by bringing enough hard rye bread for a long journey. One could always buy a little at a time, she said, for one could get it anywhere.

"Except on Lilla Nassa," I said. "But next time I think we'll bring an oven, then you'll be able to bake every day."

"That would be marvelous," said Mirre, and I think she meant it.

We hadn't shipped much water. The repairs seemed

effective. Chopping boards and clay ought perhaps to be included in every skipper's emergency outfit. Splendid! So perhaps we could continue our journey and abandon the idea of going to a repair yard.

"Lars!" shouted Pysen from the cabin. "Do come here! Sooty has got a teeny little eye. I didn't poke it, it came all by itself."

The kittens were growing daily and were now able to crawl about a bit on their own. When I went in, the little black one was sitting screwing up and blinking a newly opened little blue eye.

"They'll be climbing the rigging soon," said Rosalind, enchanted.

Knut returned. He said the island wasn't inhabited, but that there were strawberry plots which had certainly been recently picked, for only green fruit was left. He had found no water, but there were heaps of wild strawberries on the hills and he had picked enough to fill the can.

"Come ashore, all of you, and pick them," he said.

We hastily ate a meal of lightly cooked eggs and biscuits and marmalade and the remains of the last sausage, and then we took baskets and mugs and started off to pick berries.

"There are cows here," I said, "so in the evening somebody will have to come and milk them. Then we'll ask if we can buy some milk."

We found lots of wild strawberries, but not many got into the baskets because we ate most of them at once. We had quite a thirst and the strawberries helped to quench it.

The mist still lay out to seaward. We heard a steamer hooting far away. It was good to be away from all that. Saffransskär was a nice place.

In the evening a big open motorboat came putt-putting into the bay, and two girls with clinking milk pails disembarked. We hurried up and introduced ourselves and asked permission to buy milk.

"Imagine venturing out in the fog," we said.

They laughed and said they had done it so many hundred times that no fog could prevent their finding the way. And whether there was fog or not, the cows had to be milked. We went with them. Rosalind had learned to milk at a neighboring farm in Vikbolandet. She was allowed to milk one of the cows, and the girls said she did it very well. They asked us about our sailing and where we were making for, and we said that if only the fog would lift we intended to go to Möja first and telephone home, and buy provisions, and then look for a nice uninhabited island and stay there a bit. Then one of the girls said that if we were scared of the fog they could take us in tow as far as Möja. And of course we accepted very gratefully.

The other girl said, "I think you ought to go to Apelö afterward, because it's beautiful; you'll see. And you'll be quite on your own there, and there's a spring and an old barn where you can sleep if you get tired of the boat.

And there's a nice sandy beach for the little boy. There's a man who comes all the way from Västervik because he likes it so much."

"From Västervik? Not Kalle Hamper, by any chance? Because if so, we know him."

Yes, it was Kalle Hamper. He thought Apelö was the nicest island of all and on his way home always stayed there for some weeks to fish and rest for a bit. An old man in Löka owned the island, and he and Kalle Hamper were old friends.

We asked if they thought the Löka man would be annoyed if we also stayed there for a time. They said he was so nice they were certain we should be allowed to. Not many people knew the island and how lovely it was.

"Next station: Apelö," said Rosalind.

You can guess how good the milk tasted! We are all regular gluttons for milk, and we had been wanting it for so long that it seemed extra delicious. Persson drank a whole cupful and then another. Pysen kept saying, "More! More!" And then we were towed over to Möja.

Mama was so relieved that she cried into the telephone. They had been so anxious about us that they had begun to think of inquiring for *Rudolfina* over the radio. We said that we had lain sheltering in a cove and had been unable to get out in the storm, which was perfectly true. We told her that *Rudolfina* had damaged a board but that we had mended it.

We realized that Mama, being a landlubber, was thinking of an unimportant board, the chopping block, perhaps, or one in the engine cover, or part of the table, when she said, "Oh, a board? Well, that's nothing very dangerous to worry about!"

"Have you thought about coming home soon?" she asked. "It is so empty without you."

"All in good time," we said. "But you did promise us a month, didn't you?"

"I know, and you shall have it; you shall have your month out, but be very careful of yourselves."

We said we were never anything else, and that Pysen always wore his life jacket and that none of us had been bitten by adders and that everything was going fine.

Then she talked to Pysen, and he told her about Sooty's eye, and that he had drunk an enormous lot of milk and had had great fun with the bark ships and had eaten an enormous lot of strawberries.

"And tomorrow we are sailing to Apelö," said Dessi. "And you mustn't be anxious if you don't hear from us for a week or so, because there's no telephone there."

She promised to try not to worry, but said that everyone thought she and Papa were mad to have let us go off alone on such a journey, especially with Pysen. And though she hadn't really been anxious at first, or at any rate not so very much, all those worried people had upset her and she hadn't been able to help it. And the other day there had been a radio warning about storms in the

Stockholm archipelago, and that hadn't helped her fore-bodings.

We promised never to go out in *Rudolfina* in a storm, and that should one blow up while we were out we would look for a harbor as soon as possible. It was obvious, but it comforted her.

Next morning we took in oil and provisions. Then we set out for Apelö. The fog had lifted, the sun shone, and the wind was southwesterly.

CHAPTER FIFTEEN

ASK ANY OF THE young Peep-Larssons which was the best part of that summer and they would reply with one voice, "Apelö."

Apelö isn't to be found on the map, or rather, not under that name. I've called it Apelö (Apple Island) because there are wild apple trees there. We all agreed not to tell its real name to anybody, because it is Kalle Hamper's and our own little secret island, and we want to keep it to ourselves. Soon, we hope very soon, we shall sail there again. We shan't bother to visit unknown places on the way. Night and day we shall sail straight on until we see the sentinel hill with the three tall pines and the beacon, and then we shall go ashore and see if there are any traces left of Knutstorp and Kon-Tiki and the stone castle on the shore. And we shall sleep in the barn and go and see if Peter and Fiken are still living in the small lake in the wood. And we shall . . . but this book won't tell you about all that, it is only about things that have actually happened already. But if ever we become really rich we shall buy Apelö—we've decided that. There's nothing we would rather do or have.

The place I call Apelö was once two small islets separated by a little sound. This has long since become filled in and overgrown, and now consists of a long strip of salt meadowland, with alder bushes and meadow-sweet, and patches of reeds here and there. Only the opening on the western side remains. It is so deep that it will certainly be another few hundred years before that silts up and becomes land. It is a lovely little harbor, sheltered by four little islets which bear the brunt of wind and waves, but not many people find their way in because it is so small and can't be seen from the open sea, and on the chart it is just shown as a little dent in the shore.

The whole of the southern part is green and leafy with alder, birch, rowan, and hazel, with little sunny glades here and there. The beach is shelving, with a white, wavy, sandy bottom, flat, light red slabs of rock, and tiny, shallow bays. In the middle is a meadow with trees and an old gray barn, and a spring where one can get fresh water. That's where all the old gray crab apple trees grow. There is a square of moss-grown stones, too, for long ago somebody must have started building a cottage which was never finished. Or else perhaps a cottage was once there and got burned down. Wild strawberries grow all over the place, and the wild black currants that taste so good and that the local folk call tistron.

The northern part is wilder. Gray rocks, pines, and tangled firs, with blue and red whortleberry plants, linnea and ferns, huge mossy boulders and a real jungle pond of water plants, frogs, and water striders, skimming about on the surface.

Apelö became for us the island of our dreams, where we had everything we wanted. The sun shone, the perch bit, the overripe wild strawberries were sweeter there than anywhere else. We settled down on the southern part of the island, but made frequent journeys of discovery toward the north. Half an hour's row brought us to a larger island where friendly people sold us milk. Sjöström was their name. Their cows had at one time spent the summer on Apelö, but they had now moved them to an island closer to their own. They had recently cut the grass in the meadow, and the barn was full of fine, scented hay. Toward autumn they would be able to cut it again, they told us. They had a contract for the grass with the owner of the island, away in Löka, but the meadow down by the water was to remain untouched, it was to be left as it was for the wild duck.

The first thing we did when we had explored all around was to build the raft we had been longing to make. There was plenty of wood on an old tumble-down jetty—to make sure we asked the Sjöströms' permission before using it, and they laughed and said we might do what we liked with the rubbish. The only thing we had to promise was never to light a fire on the island but to stick to the primus. If we ever did want to light one, it would have to be on one of the four little islets where there was no woodland to catch fire.

Then we built our raft. It was called *Kon-Tiki*, of course, for we had all read the book. We sawed and nailed and lashed with rope ends. It turned out to be a marvelous raft, we thought. But when we launched it, though it certainly floated, the trouble was that when a couple of us climbed on board it sank under the water slightly. We puzzled a long time over how to tackle this problem, and Knut kept muttering about balsa logs and cork. So we lashed all our life belts underneath the raft, but it wasn't much good.

When I rowed over for the milk that evening, Mr. Sjöström asked how the raft was getting on, and I said we were having a little trouble in making it seaworthy. He thought for a bit and then said that during the war all the best lifesaving rafts had had air tanks to make them buoyant.

"Well, we can whistle for them, then," I said, "for how could we get air tanks here?"

Early next morning I was wakened by somebody shaking the tent and calling, "Hello!" It was Sjöström. He had come over with four old gasoline cans which he thought would do for air tanks. He helped us fasten one to each corner of the raft and lash them securely with rope, which he had with him. And this time the raft behaved as it should.

"Don't go out too far with it," he said as he left.

We said no, we were only going to use it to swim from.

That was all that we did, at first. We poled it out a bit and dived off it. We swam out, towing it behind us. We took one of the oars from the dinghy to steer with, and fastened it in a loop and maneuvered our *Kon-Tiki* about with it. It was a slow, cumbersome business and very hard work, but we all thought it much more fun than rowing in the dinghy. Once Rosalind and Knut and I poled our way all around the island and were absolutely winded by the time we got back.

Knut got Mirre to make a pirate's flag out of a pair of old black bathing trunks. He himself cut out a skull and crossbones from a torn handkerchief, and it made a fine show when Mirre had tacked them on. Then he borrowed Dessi's red scarf and knotted it over his head, so that he looked like a real sea pirate. Dessi made him earrings of dandelion stalks, and hung them over his ears with sewing thread. It looked very convincing. He had never had such fun in his life. He had a dirk of his own, and carried it between his teeth whenever he wanted to look specially fierce. I took a snapshot of him, of course, standing in all his glory, with folded arms beside the skull and crossbones on the raft.

"Say, this is a wonderful place," said Knut. "Let's stay here."

Pysen went here and there, busily picking up shells

and wading out trying to catch sticklebacks for Persson. He could swim a little way now, and this delighted him. But he was annoyed that we would so seldom have him with us on the raft. But we had very rough games on board at times, and then he was only in the way.

"I shall have a Kom-Tik of my own," he said, scowling at us, "and I shall go on it all alone with Persson. All of you are silly, so there!"

Then, one day when we were playing with the raft down by the south point, one of those sudden mists came sweeping in over the island. None of us liked it, though since we were on land there was no reason to be frightened. We left the raft where it was and went farther inland. We were in the habit of letting it lie carelessly on the shore, for the beach shelved so gently that we knew it wouldn't go far before grounding on one of the many sandbanks. And should it drift out to sea a little way, we could swim after it and easily catch up with a slow, clumsy old thing like that.

Knut and I had our tent in a hazel copse in the field, not far from the barn. We had moved the basket with Persson and the kittens there. They slept peacefully all night, but began to play so early in the morning that they roused us just when the perch were biting best.

It was time for Pysen's midday sleep. He had begun going on strike recently. He was big, he said, he could swim like the rest of us; he was a man, a real man. And real grown-up men never had a midday sleep. All the same he generally went to sleep once we got him to lie

down. I tucked him into the tent, took off his life jacket, and settled him on top of my sleeping bag. Persson and the kittens were dozing in their basket. Persson looked up for a moment, but shut her eyes again and purred when she saw Pysen.

"Have a little sleep here with Persson," I said and went away. The air was muggy and heavy because of the mist. We went into the barn and lay on the hay and talked about the spruce cabin we meant to make, and about a snake which Knut had seen near the lake. He was sure it was an adder, but when he showed us how long it was, Dessi and I said it must have been a common snake, a grass snake, or else he had exaggerated the measurements. We bickered about it for some time, and then Dessi told us some stories about snakes, and this led to other snake stories and then we started on ghost stories, for it was pretty dark inside the barn. We forgot all about the time until Mirre said, "Say, Pysen must have been awake for ages by now."

I jumped up and ran to the tent. It was perfectly quiet. I peeped in. Pysen wasn't there. I put my head right in. Yes, he had gone. And not only that but the basket and the cats had gone too. The only thing left behind was Pysen's life jacket.

I called the others and they started looking for him. We called but got no reply. I thought he might have gone down to the harbor, thinking we were out in *Rudolfina*. So I ran down there, but there was only the dinghy, lying on the shore, and no sign of Pysen. The mist lay whitey-gray and filmy out to sea. The four little islets looked like a row of gray humps.

"Hey!" I shouted to the others. "He must have gone down to the beach again." So I rushed along the beach, down to the southern point. I shouted, "Pysen!" as loudly as I could, but all I heard were other voices, also calling him. We searched through all the bushes on south Apelö, but not a sign of him did we find, nor of the cats, either.

"He can't have gone over to the north side," I said. In that case it would be serious, for there were steep rocks, there was the small lake, there were perhaps adders . . .

"He knows he's not allowed to go there," said Mirre. "But suppose he's gone and fallen into the spring?"

"Oh, no, that was the first place I went to look at," said Dessi.

Rosalind shouted from the cove. "The raft! The raft's gone!"

"Forget the raft, we can always get that later," I replied impatiently. "It can't have gone far." But Dessi caught at my arm.

"Suppose . . . suppose Pysen . . ."

"Has taken the raft, do you mean?" I said.

"Pysen!" screamed Dessi. "Answer, at once, Pysen, darling!"

We listened. There was no reply.

Rosalind came running back. She was waving something.

"Look," she said, "this was lying on the beach, just where we left the raft."

It was a little blue neck square which Pysen always wore on his head when he played pirates, like Knut. But none of us could remember whether he had been wearing it or whether we had left it lying on the beach when we went inland.

"We must divide up," I said. "Two of us take the dinghy and row out as far as we dare in the mist and look for the raft. One must stay here on the point and shout from time to time, so that the ones in the dinghy don't get lost. The other two can search the northern side of the island."

Knut and Dessi went off to do that. Mirre took on the job of guide and landmark on the point, and Rosalind and I ran down to the dinghy, calling and listening the whole time. When I saw the dinghy I stopped dead. "The oars are on the raft," I said, "I had forgotten that." We had used one oar for steering, the other for poling *Kon-Tiki*.

"Well, then, we'll swim, that will do just as well," said Rosalind. So we rushed back to the point and ran out into the water. Mirre wanted to come too, but we wouldn't let her. We needed her for a landmark.

The ground shelved for a long way out, but I had never before realized how long.

"You're out of sight!" screamed Mirre. "I can't see you anymore." And the water was still only up to our knees.

"We'll see if it's caught on any of the sandbanks, first," I said. "Hoy! Mirre! We're over here."

"Hullo—here I am," she called back.

"You take the one on the left and I'll take the one

farther out; that will save time," I said to Rosalind. "If he falls off into the water it would be over very quickly—he wasn't even wearing his life jacket. Oh, Pysen, do answer!"

I was alone in the white, woolly mist. The water was a pale leaden-gray and looked thick. I swam out toward the sandbank I knew must be quite near.

"Hullo! Here I am," came every now and then from Mirre.

I heard Rosalind answer and I answered too. I stared through the mist, waiting to see the well-known outlines of our *Kon-Tiki*, which at this moment I wished we had never built.

At last I realized I had gone past the sandbank. I understood why Mirre's calls had sounded so much fainter. I turned back and found it. But there was neither raft nor little boy. Then I swam back and forth awhile, and suddenly I saw something. My heart thudded—it couldn't be a raft, it was too small. Was it something else . . . something floating in the water?

"Pysen!" I screamed. But it was only Rosalind. And now our feet touched bottom again.

"It's simply hopeless in this mist," she said. "The raft must be quite near, you know. If only we could see it!"

"But you realize he'd have answered if he'd heard us," I said. "Either it's drifted much farther than we think, or else . . ."

"Or else he's fallen off, you mean," said Rosalind. "Oh, Lars!"

"He may be some way out in the bay," I said uncertainly. "How long were we in the barn? Two or three hours, at least. Suppose he didn't go to sleep at all but got up as soon as I'd gone. He could have gotten a long way away."

"Pysen! Where are you?"

What was that? A faint, well-known sound, growing nearer. Stonka stonka stonka.

"Dessi must have gone out in *Rudolfina* to search," I said. "It's crazy; she'll run aground. She'll never manage it. And in this mist!"

Stonka stonka stonka. We waded ashore as fast as we could.

"Run along the eastern beach and call," I said. "Pysen may have drifted past the point and gone farther along. I must get to *Rudolfina* and bring her in again."

But when I reached the bay, *Rudolfina* lay there still, and the dinghy too. I could see nobody on board. But the noise of an engine still continued. And there . . . there was a big dark shadow gliding between the islets. Now it disappeared behind the nearest rock, now it reappeared and came around it. Behind it was a long tail—what was that? A barge train, perhaps? Surely it couldn't be old *Dunkan*? Yes, it was, looking just the same as ever. And the thing behind that I dared not look at, fearing to trust my eyes? It was . . . yes, of course, the punt came first. But what was that other thing, the one at the end?

Dunkan now turned her bow inshore, hiding that other thing from me. But I knew already what it was; I had seen enough. It was *Kon-Tiki!*

Now he was going astern, Kalle Hamper. Was he alone or was anyone with him? The engine stopped, all was still, so still. I couldn't wait. I flung myself into the water and swam out and almost got *Dunkan's* great anchor dropped onto my head.

"Kalle!" I cried, "Kalle Hamper!"

He didn't hear me for the noise of the chain. Not until he had braked the capstan did he realize that somebody was shouting.

"*Rudolfina* ahoy!" he shouted.

"Kalle!" I shrieked. "Have you seen Pysen?"

Then at last I saw his bearded face, pipe in mouth, as always, as he looked over the side.

"Hullo, how are you? Nice to see you again."

"Pysen!" I called. "Do you know where Pysen is?"

"Yes," he said, "I know that all right; he's fast asleep in my bunk, and the whole family of cats with him."

Blup blup blup! sounded as my head went under and I got a gulp of water. I was so faint with relief that I let go of everything at once. When I came up I knocked against something hard that went bong! It was one of *Kon-Tiki's* air tanks. The raft had swung inward and now lay against *Dunkan's* hull. The black pirate flag drooped from its mast. I scrambled up onto the raft and Kalle stretched out a hand and pulled me aboard.

"Oh, Kalle!" I said, "to think you've found him!"

"Yes," he replied. "The little chap. Things might have gone badly with that young shrimp. I nearly ran him down without seeing him, but somehow, all of a sudden, I felt there was something there, and it was lucky that I did."

"Where did you find him?"

"A bit farther along the bay here, not very far."

"But he must have heard us calling; I can't understand why he didn't answer."

"Ah—so you called? And where are the others, then?"

"I'll find them in a minute," I said, "but I must just see him before I can really believe he's here."

We went aft. In Kalle's bunk lay Pysen, brown as a gingerbread baby, with tousled hair, sleeping as peacefully as though he had never had such a perilous adventure. Persson came up meowing. She sounded very offended. She couldn't make out why she was there at all. At the foot of the bunk lay the three kittens, asleep in a ball.

"He's a very plucky boy, that young shaver," said Kalle, quietly. "He didn't so much as whimper. He was sitting right in the middle of the raft, holding the basket with both hands. And when I hauled him up, he said, 'Persson too and the kittens too.' And bless my soul if I didn't have to take him and the cats aboard all at one go."

"Lucky it wasn't blowing," I said.

"It was perfectly calm," said Kalle. "I went in the punt, so it was easy. But go along now and find the others. This fellow will go on sleeping quite awhile yet, I'm thinking, and I'll look after him all right."

"He ran away," I said. "We thought he was asleep, and

he ran away. We usually never let him out of our sight."

"Yes, I always noticed how careful you were of him," said Kalle, "putting on his life jacket, and everything. So I was puzzled. But it's not easy to keep an eye on such a bit of quicksilver always. Well, you'll have learned not to leave him on his own again."

"I shall tether him," I said.

Then I tried to thank Kalle but couldn't. Nothing is more difficult than to thank a person properly. I just stood there and mumbled something and Kalle said, "Yes, yes, that's all right," and then he hauled in the punt so that I could row ashore.

It was some time before I could collect my poor brother and sisters and tell them Pysen had come to no harm. They could hardly believe it at first. They had already begun to fear the worst. Dessi never said a word. She went down on to the beach and stayed there, sitting on a rock for quite a time. When she came back, she said, "It would have been so ghastly if the worst had happened that I don't think I could have faced going home to Papa and Mama again. Because it was all my fault. I was responsible."

"We all were," I said.

"But I am the eldest. Oh, if you knew how awful it is sometimes, being the eldest when one is such a scatterbrain as I am. But I am so thankful, at this moment, that it hurts!"

"Well, cheer up," I said. "Come on and let's go aboard and find Pysen and the cats and see Kalle."

"Look, there's *Kon-Tiki*," said Knut when he caught sight of the raft. "Fine raft, anyway; it's been out on a long voyage and come home safe again."

"And how good of Kalle to salvage it," said Rosalind. "What can we do for him? He ought to have a gold watch or something."

"I want to hug him," said Mirre, drying her red, swollen eyes.

"We all feel like that," said Rosalind, "but perhaps he wouldn't like it."

"He'll have to put up with it," said Mirre, blowing her nose. "He must know we've got to hug someone now."

He knew, all right; he wasn't so dumb.

"Well, well, that's all right," said he, patting Mirre on the back. "Everything's all right now, all's well that ends well. And I think you'll take even more care now of that little shrimp."

"I'll paint a thousand baskets for you," said Dessi.

"Thanks, that would be fine. A pity I haven't any left to paint. I've been out at Svartlöga and Rödlöga and got rid of every single one. But when I come out next year perhaps I can pop in at Bråviken for a bit and get some painted then."

"As many as you could possibly want," said Dessi.

We went to the little green cabin astern and pushed open the door. It creaked, for the hinges needed oiling. Pysen stretched, rubbed his eyes with his fist, and sat up. He couldn't quite make out where he was. Then he caught sight of us crowding in at the door and began to remember everything.

"Good morning," said Kalle Hamper.

"Good morning," he replied. "Where's Persson?"

"Just gone out," I answered. "She wants to go ashore and scratch."

"We've been on Kom Ticken, me and Persson," said Pysen, his face shining. "And Sooty, too, and Whitenose too and Graytip too have been out on Kom Ticken. And one oar fell in the water."

"Pysen," said Dessi, hugging him, "tell me. Didn't you hear us calling you?"

"Yes," he replied, "you shouted 'Py-sen, Py-sen!' Like that."

"Well, but why in the wide world didn't you answer, ducky?"

"I don't bellow, noho," said he, "you do. And then you say I do!"

Dessi laughed and cried at the same time. Kalle hid behind the doorpost and laughed so that his pipe fell on the deck.

"Pysen, darling," said Dessi when she had pulled herself together a little, "remember that you must always answer when anyone calls you."

"I'm not going to bellow, noho," said Pysen. "Men don't bellow. Lars said so."

"From now on, Pysen," I said, "you can roar and bellow as much as ever you like. And men always answer when anyone calls them. They answer 'yes, here I am!'"

He gazed at me to see if I was in earnest.

"Yes!" he screamed, "here I am! Was that right?"

"A bit louder, perhaps," I said.

"YES, HERE I AM!" he shrieked at the top of his voice.

"A real opera singer," said Kalle Hamper.

"That's splendid," said I.

"Can I have some milk now, and something to eat? And Persson, too?"

"That you can, ducky," said Mirre.

CHAPTER SIXTEEN

HOW LOVELY everything was! How happy we were!
What a glorious time we had! To have Kalle Hamper
with us and that we were all going to stay there for a bit
was the nicest thing that could have happened.

Kalle was the best possible companion. He knew about
everything and could do anything, and nobody knew the
archipelago as well as he did. He found our missing oar
in an inlet; he showed us a grotto in the cliffs to the
north of Apelö and a sea eagle's nest on one of the
rugged islands to the northeast.

He took Rosalind and me to the small lake in the
woods and introduced us to Peter and Fiken, a pair of old
grass snakes that he had known for many years. He gave
them milk and cod's roe in an old anchovy can, and they
came swimming across the lake and took the food just as
if they had been ducks on a pond. We had been to the
lake lots of times, but it was only when Kalle was with us
that the snakes came so close.

"Peter is so greedy," he said. "Look how he guzzles.
But Fiken, she's a little lady, she is. Look how she nods
and bows her head, and see how intelligent her eyes
are."

"It must have been Peter or Fiken that Knut saw," I said. "He took it for an adder. He thought of coming to look for it again and killing it, but Rosalind said adders had a right to live too."

"Look at them, and see what adders don't look like," said Kalle. "Adders never have those golden patches by their ears. Fiken, then, come along, my pretty!" And he took a grass stem and tickled Fiken's neck, and she wriggled and reared her head in pleasure, staring curiously at us with her glittering eyes.

Rosalind couldn't tear herself away. "Just think," she said, "Kalle is a snake charmer." Then Kalle told us that he had had a tame grass snake at home in Småland when he was a boy.

"It was like a cat," he said. "I used to have it on my knee. But then our hedgehog came along and did it in one fine day. And it was only because it was jealous of it, because I used to give it new milk and the hedgehog only got skim! And I suppose he thought that unfair, because he did keep the house free of rats. But one can find hedgehogs anywhere, whereas I was the only chap who had a tame grass snake, so I thought it ought to have the best."

Kalle slept in the barn; he loved the scent of the hay. One night Knut and I slept there too, and it was then I told Kalle about our mishap at Lilla Nassa.

"Dear, dear, that might have been a very bad thing," said Kalle.

The next day he wanted to have a look at the leak. He

inspected it first from the inside, and then he started up the engine and took *Rudolfina* to the inlet and up onto the sandbank there. Then we pulled and hauled and he dragged her a bit more and we got her up far enough for him to see the bit of planking that I had screwed on. He tapped it and pushed it and felt it, then he murmured, "They've made a fine job of this, have those kids. It holds, yes, it holds all right; a neat bit of work."

"The patch looks a bit rough," I said. "But we had nothing else we could use. And anyway, the water doesn't come in anymore. But I should feel ashamed for them to see it in a shipyard."

"There's nothing to be ashamed of," said Kalle. "It's very ingenious and clever when you remember the little you had to work with. I couldn't have done any better myself."

"We're in for a difficult time when we go home with the boat in this condition," said Dessi. "The worst of it is that they'll never let us out on our own again, perhaps, after this."

"Anyone can run aground," said Kalle. "Everyone who sails has done so at one time or another. Why, I couldn't say how many times I have scraped a hidden rock myself."

"You have?" I asked.

"Bless me, yes. I've been here with *Dunkan* time and time again, summer after summer for twenty-two years, but it still happens occasionally. The archipelago isn't an easy place to sail in. One August a year or so ago I came in to Svartlöga in pouring rain late one evening and skidded over rocks, so I know how slippery it feels on pigs' backs."

That was a comfort. If it could happen to Kalle Hamper, fine seaman that he was . . .

"But I got off. I couldn't see a hand's length in front of me and dared not go on farther, so I dropped anchor haphazard and lay there all night. In the morning, when I came out I saw I was lying right in the middle of a stony field, like. Big and little rocks stuck up out of the water all around, and under the water were even more of them."

"Oooh!" said Mirre.

"I never thought I'd get out with a whole skin, and if it had come on to blow old *Dunkan* would have been a wreck in no time. But my one bit of luck was that it stayed calm. I went out in the punt and sounded a bit here and there and found a way out. But how I managed to get into that pickle and only scrape a bit of varnish off the craft I can never make out."

"You were lucky," I said.

"I certainly was, that time. But I haven't always been. Losing the propeller and getting stuck on a sandbank, and lying helpless, drifting before the wind, with a broken rudder. You have to reckon with such things if you want to go to sea. As long as you don't lose your head you can generally get out of your difficulties. Though storms and gusty winds are not to be played with, and of course fog is the worst of all. It's so treacherous. Don't ever go out in fog. And if you get caught in one, make for the nearest shelter or anchor where you are if you can."

"I never want to see mist again in all my life," said Dessi.

"One forgets so easily when one is young," said Kalle, knocking out his pipe against *Rudolfina*'s side. "But talking of leaks, you've mended that one so well that I don't think you need bother about getting to a yard just at present. I think you'll manage to get home all right with her just as she is. But when you lay her up in the autumn, of course you'll have to get it seen to. You won't have to have a whole new plank, only a bit put in, from here to here"—he pointed with his pipe to a spot each side of the chopping board—"so that the new piece extends far enough to make it perfectly safe."

"Will it cost a lot?" I asked.

"Well, a bit more than a chopping board and a can of putty, but not more than your Papa will be able to manage quite comfortably. When you buy a boat you must expect to have a few expenses in connection with her, and, being a businessman, he'll have realized that."

"He could stop our pocket money for a bit," said Knut.

Yes, it was actually Knut saying that. He was more scared than any of us that Papa might get rid of *Rudolfina* when he knew all that had happened.

Kalle Hamper had been tattooed. He had a magnificent woman on one arm and a compass rose on the other, and on his chest was an absolute masterpiece in blue and red, a four-masted barque in full sail. "Euphrosyne" was written in a half circle above it, right under Kalle's chin. Knut greatly admired this splendid tattooing, and one fine day he got Dessi to paint *Rudolfina* on his own chest, all in oils and many brilliant colors, with sail hoisted and signal flags flying, and Knut himself at the tiller. He squirmed and giggled while she was painting, for he was very ticklish. But his "tattooing" was so well done that it really was a shame it couldn't last like Kalle's. He was very careful of it, and the first day he would only swim on his back so as not to wear it out unnecessarily.

After a while Kalle helped us build the cabin of spruce fir that we had been talking about for so long. We built it under a bushy, giant fir in the northern part of the woods, and it was so well hidden under the fir's own trailing branches that one really had to know where it was in order to be able to find it. One could see that Kalle was a basket maker, for the sides were woven like one of his own potato baskets. It was so thick and firm that Pysen could climb right onto the roof without falling through.

"What shall we call it?" we wondered.

"Pysen House," said Kalle.

"Why not Knut House?" I said, for Knut had worked hardest over it.

It became Knutstorp. There is a castle of that name, I think, and Knut thought our lovely cabin was just as good. We made a table out of a tree stump and brought in stones for chairs, and Kalle treated us to coffee and we sat there eating rusks and buttered gingerbread. Of course I took a photograph, but it didn't come out because the inside of the cabin was so dark.

Down on the southern side of the point we built sand castles for Pysen. There he stayed, digging and making pies. Persson and the three kittens were with him. The kittens had already begun to play a little, and Rosalind looked after them and the rest of us looked after Pysen. A little way off from there we had a small jetty of stones going right out into the water and a real little stone castle.

We had long outstayed the week which we had thought of allowing ourselves on Apelö. It was hard to decide to tear ourselves away. Our parents couldn't really be anxious, for we had all written letters and sent them when we went to fetch the milk, for there were steamers that called at neighboring jetties. And we had nothing to worry about on our own account. We could buy as many herrings as we wanted, and one day Sjöström said that Kalle and some of us might go with him and take up the cod nets. Rosalind and Knut and I went. The catch had been good and we brought three magnificent cod back to Mirre, who cooked them in a Peep saucepan and made egg sauce to go with them. We all—Persson included—had two marvelous meals.

Kalle took some of the roe to Peter and Fiken. We all went along to watch them eat it. But evidently they were

scared at seeing so many of us and kept away. Not until
the others tired, and only Rosalind and Kalle were left,
did they come out and have a feast as well.

But our month was drawing to an end; and Kalle, too,
started saying that Vendla was waiting for him to fetch
her from Nynäshamn now.

We had a feast on the last day. We rowed out to the
four little islets and lit a bonfire on each of them. Then
we sat down on the biggest—the Limpet, it is called—
and ate grilled herrings and baked potatoes in the ashes.
Kalle enjoyed it all as much as we did.

"I'm a boy once more!" he cried, turning a somersault,

so that his cap fell off and we saw that he really did have hair and hadn't been scalped as Knut believed.

Then we got him to sing sea chanteys for us. He sang one about a Danish brig, the *Skulda*, which sailed out to sea and sank, and when he thought Dessi looked a bit melancholy he cheered her up with "Blow, Boys, Blow for California." Mirre was enthralled by "Little Edwin" and wouldn't rest until she had learned it by heart. It has become one of her three favorite songs and she always sings it when washing up. She begins in a long-drawn mournful wail:

> Little Edwin has gone far away,
> He sails the stormy billow,
> I weep for him every day
> My salt tears bedewing my pillow.

Then, rather more dramatically,

> Said her mother to proud Emily,
> Why waste on a sailor your heart?
> Your life you are throwing away,
> From young Edwin 'tis better to part.

When Emily talks about weaving garlands and laying them on Edwin's grave, he, who lies in the cold ocean, Mirre's voice quavers, so that I always say, "Oh, dry up, Mirre." But she takes no notice. She allows her Emily to fall to the ground in a swoon, but to come round to rather better news, and then she bellows so that the glasses rattle on the shelves:

> Little Edwin was reefing the sail,
> He slipped and fell into the sea
> But was borne to the shore by the gale
> And thus he reached harbor safely.

The last verse goes at a galloping pace.

> Little Edwin is happy once more,
> He knows neither sorrow nor pain,
> With his Emily safely ashore
> They will never be parted again.

The herrings were eaten, the bonfires burned out, and we had to turn in so as to be up early next morning. Everything was packed and stowed away, the tent was aboard, *Rudolfina* was trim and shipshape.

"We'll keep together as long as we can," said Kalle. "You can have the engine going, so we needn't separate just yet."

"Right," said I, "as long as there isn't a favorable wind, because we'd have to sail then."

"No chance of that," said Kalle. "If there's a wind it will be a contrary one. You very seldom get a northerly or nor'east wind in July."

CHAPTER SEVENTEEN

KALLE ROUSED US when it was only half past five. He was lying in the water with his cap on, hanging on to a rope alongside *Dunkan*, splashing himself awake and singing,

> Rouse up, rouse up the starboard watch,
> Rouse up, rouse up the helmsman.

It was the only time I saw Kalle swim.

"What did I tell you?" he asked as I came out. "It's sou'west, and precious little at that, so there'll be no sailing."

The mallards in the bay came swimming along, quacking. They expected him to offer them something nice to eat. But we took a hurried dip and put on our clothes. Then we had coffee aboard *Dunkan*, and while the others rowed back I washed up, and Kalle started busying himself with his engine. I had just finished hanging up the cups in the galley when he got the stonka stonka going, but just afterward something seemed to go wrong; it turned over for a while, then stopped. I put my head out.

"Did you try too soon?" I asked.

Then something amazing happened. The great flywheel in front of the engine came adrift and fell to the bottom of the boat, landing with a thud that shook the whole craft. Kalle and I stared. Neither of us had ever seen such a thing before. Kalle took his pipe out of his mouth and said something short and sharp.

"What on earth happened?" I asked. "What made it do that?"

"Axle gone," said Kalle. "Couldn't be anything else. Lucky the engine stopped, otherwise the whole thing would have gone right through the bottom."

"Is a flywheel as heavy as that?"

"It weighs two or three hundred kilos," he replied.

"What are you going to do, then?"

"Do? Well, I can't do a thing by myself."

"Couldn't we . . ." I began, but he shook his head and examined his Bruzaholmer.

"This will be a job for a crane," he said. "I'll have to get her to a repair yard—but how?"

"We can tow you," I said, "*Rudolfina*'s marvelous at towing."

"Hm. Well, as far as I can see that may be the only thing to do. Yes, look, boy, now I see what happened. Here's an old crack that's been there goodness knows how long—before my time—and rust has gotten in and gradually eaten away the metal until the whole thing corroded. Well, well, it served many a man faithfully for years. You can't expect an axle to last longer than a man.

And one must be thankful that it happened when it did and not in a rough sea or anything."

"Can it be mended?" I asked.

"Bless me, yes. It will have to be welded and then turned on a lathe, I expect, before it's fit for use again. But first we shall have to take down the whole blessed contraption. Let me see, I know a chap in Dalarö with a good boatyard. I can do most of it myself, for that matter, once I get this lifted out of the way. Do you think you'll be able to get me all the way down to Dalarö?"

"Right on to Västervik if you like," I answered. "*Rudolfina*'s an old tugboat, as you know."

"Good. But you're going to find it boring, for *Dunkan* will slow down your speed, you know."

"That doesn't matter. We've still four days to go before our month's up, so we can take it easy."

"Lucky for me you were here," said Kalle.

"Well, wasn't it lucky for us that you were here, a while back?"

"Don't talk rubbish, my lad. And now let's see how we're going to maneuver to get both our frigates out of here without a hitch. I think you'll have to go around *Dunkan*, first, and face upwind before I can pass a line."

Rosalind came across in the dinghy to fetch me and saw the damage the flywheel had caused. Then began a fairly tricky bit of work, but Kalle directed it and told us what to do. *Dunkan* was in our way when we had to move out, and we had to take a line from her and row ashore with it and tug until we got her turned. Then we could only just squeeze by, and when we had *Dunkan* in tow she tried at first to pull herself and us in quite the wrong direction. But when at last we managed to get away from the rocks and get up a little speed, matters went better. Kalle stood at *Dunkan's* helm, I at *Rudolfina's*.

"She's going awfully slowly," said Mirre. "Still, she's going."

"How many knots are we doing?" inquired Knut, attempting a "spit-log" to time the speed.

"Possibly two," I said. We usually made about five.

"Two and a half," said Knut. "At least two and a half."

The wind was right ahead, but actually there wasn't much of it, which was fortunate; otherwise we should have gone even more slowly, for *Dunkan* was an efficient wind trap.

Stonka stonka stonka, said our engine, and the journey took us through the islands north of Möja and beyond Möja Sound down toward Kanholmen. We were going slower than we would had we been on our own, beating upwind, but nobody complained. We were so glad to be able to do something to help Kalle Hamper. And somehow when you are towing you feel that for once in a way you are doing a really useful job. We had arranged with Kalle not to stop anywhere but go straight on to Dalarö.

Out beyond Kanholmen the wind abated. Then the girls got a meal ready and opened a can of mutton and cabbage which we had left to the last, because Pysen and Knut weren't very fond of cabbage. When the smell of cooking cabbage began mingling with the fumes of the engine, Kalle set up a bellowing and came forward from *Dunkan's* stern.

"Don't tell me that's cabbage you've got there, youngsters," he roared. "That's my favorite dinner."

"Come over and have some with us," shouted Mirre. "We've got lots."

"I'd come like a shot," he answered, "But I can't leave the helm."

"I'll stop a minute so the girls can bring you a bite of food over in the dinghy," I said.

We did so. Rosalind took the saucepan with the cabbage and mutton and climbed into the dinghy, and Kalle met her with a delighted grin. Then he ate until, as he said, he sweated.

"That was something like a dinner," he said.

Mirre hurriedly fried up a little batter, and Knut and Pysen were very pleased. They much prefer pancakes and sugar to mutton and cabbage.

It was almost six in the evening by the time we reached Dalarö. We went with Kalle to the shipyard where he knew some of the men. And though they had stopped work for the day, he had only to show his face among them and push his cap back an inch from his forehead, as he did when greeting you, for everything to become possible.

"You see, Vendla's sitting waiting in Nynäshamn and

she's been expecting me for some days, and now goodness knows how long she'll have to wait."

"Oh, it oughtn't to take so very long," said the foreman. "Come and help me with the crane so we can get up that great millstone you've got there. We can manage the welding here, but you'll have to take the axle into town by bus and get it turned."

Knut and I went to see if we could buy a couple of loaves and some other things that we needed. We came to a shop just as it was about to close. There was a lady there, carrying a string bag.

"I've promised to give a few little fancy articles for a grab bag at the charity fête, you know," she said. "Have you anything suitable? It doesn't matter what, particularly."

"Toothbrushes, perhaps?" said the girl behind the counter, "or paper table napkins? We haven't got anything else, really, unless you'd care for something in the eating line."

"What a pity," said the lady. "The other shops are all closed. Toothbrushes and paper napkins are so dull, I think. What had I better do? I asked my husband to get a few little things in town today, but of course he forgot and came back empty-handed."

I saw Knut prick up his ears. He glanced at me. Well, why not? I nudged him and nodded.

"Excuse me," he said to the lady, "but I've got a whole lot of little things suitable for a grab bag."

"I must close now if there's nothing else you want," said the girl behind the counter.

But the lady became interested, and she and Knut went on talking outside in the road. I took my loaves and other things and went off, and shortly afterward Knut came tearing after me.

"You'll see, she'll buy some of my things," he said. "I'll get the briefcase and go to her house with it now."

Down in the boatyard Kalle and the foreman had gotten the flywheel and engine hoisted up and were in the process of dismantling the axle. We were also going to lie alongside the shipyard overnight. Knut was away some time and then came rushing back, delighted.

"Every single thing gone!" he said. "I could have sold three times as much, then think what I should have made!"

We had our evening meal and then Dessi and Mirre went ashore to have a look at Dalarö. They were away a good long time, and we others turned in. Just for fun we took their bunks and thought they would go and sleep in the fo'c'sle just for one night. They came tiptoeing aboard at last.

"Hush, they're asleep already," whispered Dessi.

They undressed in the dark and were just climbing into bed when Mirre yelled to high heaven because my sleeping bag moved just as she was about to get into it.

"The ladies will be sleeping in the fo'c'sle tonight," said Knut. "Their sleeping bags are there, all ready."

"Oh, my goodness, what a fright I got," said Mirre. "Yes, of course I'll sleep in the fo'c'sle if you think there's room. I'll manage somehow, even if I have to twist myself into loops." Mirre is our giantess. I may not have told you.

But Dessi said, "All right, but, Knut, we've got one or two little presents for you—here they are."

"Presents? What presents?" asked Knut. "Light the lantern so that I can see what they are." Dessi lit it.

"Oh!" he exclaimed, staring at what lay in his hand. It was two little well-known green gauze bags.

"They're all yours, Knut dear," said Dessi. "You used to collect glass beads, didn't you?"

"Where did you get hold of these?" he asked.

"We've been to a charity fête," said Mirre. "We got these out of a grab bag, for a krona. Nice, eh?"

Knut leapt up. "I shall throw them into the water," he said, "Then I'll be sure of having seen the last of them."

"Oh no, I don't think you ought to," said Dessi. "Keep them until Little O is old enough not to eat them. Little girls always love threading beads."

"Well," said Knut, "I'll keep them until she's five or six and then give them to her for a Christmas present."

"He who saves shall grow rich," murmured Rosalind, from her corner. "When you're rich I hope you'll remember your poor old brothers and sisters and give them an occasional ice cream."

"You shall all have ice creams tomorrow," said Knut, "chocolate ones."

"We called them up at home, too," continued Dessi. "Everything's O.K. We told them about Kalle and the flywheel, and Papa said we needn't go home tomorrow but might wait here so we can be with Kalle till he goes down to Bråviken." She didn't say that she had asked if we might do that because she felt safer when Kalle was about, in case of accidents. But I knew she had, all the same.

Next morning Kalle went in to Stockholm with his axle. We went out to Askfatet, where sailing boats generally anchor. We didn't want to take up room in the shipyard, where they were already rather crowded.

In the evening I went to the boatyard just as he returned. He had been lucky. He had met an old mate of his in the workshop there, he said. He had old friends everywhere.

It took the whole next day to set up the engine again. I hung around and watched. I thought it might be very useful to get to know as much as possible about an old Bruzaholmer. One fine day something of that sort might happen to us. In the evening the engine was lifted aboard and made fast and then came the exciting moment for testing it. But all went well. Stonka stonka stonka, it went, and stonka stonka stonka echoed from the other side.

"There we are!" said Kalle cheerfully. "In the morning we'll be able to get away from here."

CHAPTER EIGHTEEN

WE REACHED Nynäshamn in five hours. There we were all invited to Vendla's sister's, Mrs. Fredriksson. She was much better now, but very sad over Vendla's approaching departure. When she heard us talking about the kittens she wanted to have one in order to console herself, and since Aunt Bella had said that in any case she could only keep one, we let Mrs. Fredriksson choose between Whitenose and Graytip. We couldn't think of parting with Sooty. He was the liveliest of them all, jet black, without a single white hair, and it was already obvious that he was going to be Rosalind's own special cat.

Mrs. Fredriksson chose Whitenose and was so delighted with him that she forgot to cry because Vendla was going away. But she had already been crying for several days, so she told us. She was certainly devoted to her sister. And I believe she really enjoyed crying, too!

We had lunch at a properly laid table. It felt unusual and important. We had roast chicken and raspberry cake. And when Knut had finished with a chicken bone he threw it out of the window without thinking. He didn't remember that we weren't at sea and was very embarrassed when he realized what he had done. But Vendla's sister laughed until she had to leave the table. Vendla herself had a toothache, and sat there with a swollen face, but she laughed, too, until she cried.

That night we anchored outside Trehörningen again.

Cats can obviously not count up to three, for Persson didn't notice that one of her children had disappeared. Mama ought to have been a cat!

We had intended to leave pretty early the following morning. But at about seven Kalle came and said Vendla's toothache had become so bad that she would have to go to a dentist first. And there she sat in the waiting room, half the morning, so we couldn't weigh anchor before midday.

"Dr. Wood was a quicker worker," said Knut when at last Vendla returned.

As it was calm and simply boiling hot, and the swallows were flying high, we asked Kalle if we mightn't go out to sea for one last time. We wanted to see the Landsort lighthouse from close up.

"Yes," he said, "it wouldn't be much out of our way. It'll just mean about a couple of hours extra if we go there, and we can afford that. We won't go ashore, for the harbor's tricky there, at least for a boat *Dunkan*'s size. But we'll take a trip around Öja and look at the lighthouse from all sides—we can do that, anyhow. We'll have a sailing race there."

"One under power," said Mirre. For we were going to use our engine, too; we shouldn't have managed the trip in time otherwise.

Kalle led. *Dunkan* could make greater speed than we could. But it wasn't a very serious sort of race, for when we got too far behind, Kalle slackened speed and waited for us.

The sea glittered white in the strong sunlight. One couldn't look at it for long without being blinded. When we got out a little way we became conscious of a sort of heaving swell which bore us along very pleasantly. I had handed over the tiller to Knut, and Dessi sat close beside him to keep watch should anything happen. I half lay on the fo'c'sle deck, listening to the little rushing sound made by *Rudolfina's* bow cleaving the water. The engine stonka'd behind me, and a mingled smell of kerosene and coffee from *Dunkan* was sometimes wafted toward us. The barge pushed through the water, cumbersome and heavy. Against the green cuddy astern I saw Kalle's everlasting yachting cap like a round black inkblot, and from the chimney stack on the roof streamed a thin thread of light blue smoke.

I closed my eyes. Through the lids the brilliant daylight showed reddish gold like apricot jam. Nothing makes me so happy and at the same time drowsy as to lie in the sun like that. I dozed off and dreamed a number of queer little muddled, disjointed dreams. One of them I remember even now. I was mashing together strawberries and tow in an anchovy can and feeding Peter and

Fiken with it in Aunt Bella's laundry room. And both snakes ate and squirmed until I grew quite dizzy watching them, and fell right down on the floor under the mangle.

I woke up while I was doing this, and there we were, right opposite Landsort, jibing so that I smacked up against the gunwale and almost fell into the water.

There stood the white lighthouse, high as a church, upon the rocks, and below it lay the cottages, clustered together like a flock of frightened chickens around a hen. People came out of the cottages and waved to us and we waved back.

"Would you like to live here all the year round," I asked Dessi, "on an island in the middle of the sea, where it's often stormy, and you can never go out to the pictures, or meet new people, or do any trading, or go in a trolley?"

"I don't know that I should always like to live there," she said, "but I should for a time, anyway. And the people there aren't any lonelier than we have been for most of the time during this past month. They've got their own families with them, you know. But to be a lighthouse keeper living quite isolated in a lighthouse, without any neighbors, that might not always be much fun."

"Not always? Do you mean that sometimes it *would* be nice?"

"Of course," she replied. "Everyone needs to be alone sometimes. It gives one time to think a bit. Otherwise one talks from morning till night, like a record player, and in between times stands about and—"

"Listens to other record players, do you mean?" asked Rosalind, who was standing close by. It was appropriate, for just at that moment Mirre started on the third verse of "Little Edwin" for the fourth time. It ended with "Mid the blossoms I'll lie in my grave."

"Stop!" I shouted. "Turn off that record, Mirre, we're all sick of it."

"But I'm not," said Mirre, continuing unperturbed.

Kalle signaled us from *Dunkan* and pointed up to the mast. We didn't know what he meant, so he came toward us and shouted above the noise of both engines, "If I were you I'd hoist a bit of sail now; we're heading due west."

"Right," said Dessi.

"You'll go ahead of us now," shouted Kalle, "but we'll meet in Sävsundet and put in there for the night."

We agreed.

"Your birthday cove, Pysen," said Rosalind.

"Can I have more cake, then?" he asked delightedly, "and another duckling? And shall we wave all the little flags?"

"I think you'll get some blueberries," said Rosalind. "They'll be ripe enough by now."

We set sail and headed out from Öja. The wind was fair. Soon Landsort's lighthouse was no bigger than the plaster churches they used to sell in the Great Market Christmas Fair, when we lived in Stockholm.

Kalle was right; we passed *Dunkan* and reached Säv-sundet three quarters of an hour before she did. We had already managed to cook potatoes and lay places for our guests, the Hampers, as well as ourselves, by the time they stonka'd into the bay.

Pysen gave us no peace until he had hoisted the signal flags, and since it would probably be our last meal with Kalle and Vendla, we thought it appropriate to make it rather a celebration.

"We haven't such fine flags as those," said Vendla, whose face was now normal once more. "But in the night, when I couldn't sleep for the toothache, I baked you one of those cakes you liked so much. I thought I would give it to you when we said good-bye, but perhaps it won't keep as long as that, so here it is, and help yourselves!"

And in this way Pysen got cake again in his birthday cove, after all.

After dinner we went ashore and picked blueberries.

"Dessi," said Kalle as we were on our way, "did you like that lighthouse back there?"

"Yes, of course I did," she said.

"I knew you would, you are the kind who would. You youngsters have a fine big sister."

"Kalle," said Dessi, "do we have to wait until tomorrow to leave?"

"Have to wait? Are you beginning to long for home, lassie?"

"Of course they are all longing for home," said Vendla. "One always does when one's nearly there."

Then I realized, all of a sudden, that I was rather looking forward to getting back home, in spite of the lovely holiday we had had.

"The best part of being away is the coming home, people say," said Kalle. "Yes, I think, too, that it will be good to get home to Mistermåla and start work again."

"It will be nice to see how much Little O has grown, and hear if she has learned any new words," said Dessi.

"And then see Laban and Lotta," said Rosalind.

"And tell the dye manager about everything that has happened," said Knut.

"It certainly will be nice to sleep in a proper bed again," said Mirre, who had been somewhat cramped aboard.

"Yes, though that wasn't exactly what I meant," said Dessi. "I just meant that I think it would be such fun if we could leave tonight and navigate by lights. We've never actually spent a whole night at sea so far."

"I've nothing against that idea," said Kalle. "Vendla can go to bed, and so can the young shavers, too. I often navigate by the lights—they are so reliable. But don't you think you youngsters would get sleepy?"

"Pooh! We can sleep after we get home," said I.

Dessi said she could promise not to fall asleep at the helm. But Mirre said, "I think we'll set out, but I shall turn in, and Knut and Pysen likewise."

"Not I!" said Knut.

"Not me, noho," said Pysen, "because I must pull down the darling little flags first."

"Yes, ducky, you shall do that, of course," said Mirre.

"I'm not ducky, I'm a man, so there," said Pysen.

"Yes, ducky, of course you're a man," said Mirre.

"If we navigate by lights there's no hurry," said Kalle. "If we start round nineish we'll reach the entrance to Brå-viken at dawn and say good-bye there. Shall we do that?"

"Yes," we all replied.

"I think I'll go aboard and start tidying up and packing," said Mirre, "then that will be done with."

On the stroke of nine we set off. The evening was warm. Midges in huge swarms came round *Rudolfina*, but after we had gone a little way they disappeared for the most part. The wind had died down and *Dunkan* led the way. The evenings had already begun getting darker; it would soon be August.

"It will be bright starlight," said Dessi.

"This time tomorrow we shall have ridden Laban and Lotta to water," said Rosalind to me.

"And told Papa and Mama all our adventures," I said.

"Mama will take the one about Pysen hardest," said Dessi.

"Yes," I replied, "and it was my fault. I oughtn't to have left him alone in the tent."

"We all knew he was alone there," said Rosalind, "so we were all equally guilty."

"Never mind whose fault it was," said Mirre, yawning. "The chief thing is that we shall all get home safe and sound. I think it's very clever of us not to have lost anyone during a whole month. We've done well, though I do say it myself."

"Hear hear," said I.

"We must light the lanterns," said Dessi. "They've lit up aboard *Dunkan*."

"I did fill them," said Mirre. "Good night, all. Pysen's asleep already, with the cats. Tell me when it's time to wave good-bye to Kalle."

"You've already said good-bye to him and Vendla."

"I can wave a bit, anyhow. Look how nice he is, he's making certain not to get too far away from us. I think he's marvelous."

She closed the shutter after her and hung the mosquito net over the open door.

Ahead of us went *Dunkan*, sure as a bloodhound on the trail, nosing her way between the buoys in the dark-

ening channel. The lighthouses started winking, one after
another. For the most part we sat thinking how beautiful
it was, and I shone the flashlight occasionally on the
chart to follow our course. But we knew that where Kalle
led we might safely follow.

Knut obstinately insisted on staying up and timing the
lighthouses' flashes; some were at three-second intervals,
some at six. But at last he began nodding where he
sat.

"You can have my bunk tonight," said Dessi, "because
I won't be using it."

Then he turned in. Dessi's bunk was much sought
after, for it was the most comfortable. After a time I
peeped through the shutter. Knut was asleep with all his
clothes on.

"You'll have to help him," said Dessi, "or he'll feel
awful when he wakes up."

I took off his shoes and jacket, loosened his belt,

and came up again. Then we sat silent, Dessi, Rosalind, and I. The stars sprang out in the sky like the little white flowers on Aunt Bella's myrtle. *Dunkan*'s lantern aft shone yellow-white. We went in the white beams of the lights.

"Lovely!" I said to Dessi. She nodded.

"Mm," she said.

"You must wish you could paint this."

"It isn't necessary to paint it," she replied, "or write about it, either."

"No?" I said. (Because, for my part, I often think it necessary to write.)

"The chief thing is that one sees it," she said. "Kalle was awfully good to do this with us."

"Look out," I said, "you're steering for the red light. Keep to the white one."

"You take the tiller if you will," she said, and I took it.

"Shall I get some cake? There's heaps left," said Rosalind.

As we ate we came to a long open stretch of water.

"It was here that we met the steamer," said Rosalind. "I mean, it was here Knut went overboard."

We felt cold shivers down our backs.

"Well, anyway, he's down there, lying safe asleep," I said.

We went past Korpholmen's lighthouse, and when we ported the helm and came first into the red and then the green sector, we saw the three chimneys of Oxelösund's

Ironworks rear three black pillars against the starry sky. Then we were out into the white sector again and the shore melted into shadow. I looked at the time. Half past twelve already!

"What can we do for Kalle?" I said.

"Yes, what?" said both the girls at once.

"We can man the side and cheer," I said. "That's about the only thing we can find to do."

Half an hour later we were out in open water once more. Over the islands to the northeast a faint light was beginning to show already. The stars were paler.

Ahead of us *Dunkan* slackened speed. Kalle signaled with a lantern. Rosalind crept in and wakened Mirre. She came out with a bathrobe over her nightgown.

We went up to *Dunkan*.

"Good-bye, young shrimps!" cried Kalle. "Here you are again at Bråviken, now."

The three girls manned the side as the boats glided alongside each other. I couldn't leave the helm.

"Hurrah for Kalle Hamper! Long live Kalle! Three cheers for Kalle!" I cried.

"Hurrah! Hurrah! Hurrah!"

Kalle sounded the hooter in salute and took off his cap. Yes, actually took it off and waved it.

"Thanks for your company," he cried. "Come soon and see Vendla and me in Mistermåla, all of you."

"Come to us!" we yelled.

"Now you've got a bit of a wind," he called.

A breeze ruffled the water, and *Rudolfina's* pennant

fluttered. *Dunkan* glided astern. Now Kalle started up his engine.

"Hoist the mains'l, girls," I said and stopped the engine. "We shall be home in two or three hours."

We waved again. Kalle waved his hand, but now he had put on his cap again.

Stonka stonka stonka sounded faintly from far-away *Dunkan*.

Then we set sail.